I WAS TREMBLING . . .

The thunder rumbled. The window frames rattled. The lights flickered out. Derek Hawke stood directly in front of me. His face was inches from mine. He seized my arms.

"What nonsense has she been saying?" he demanded. "Tell me!"

"Let me go!" I whispered. I tried to break free, but his hands merely tightened their grip. I shook my head. In another moment I would be screaming. He swung me into his arms. His lips bore down on mine, and there was nothing but sensation—sharp, violent sensation that crushed me under its merciless impact.

Derek Hawke released me abruptly. He stood looking at me while crashes of thunder deafened both of us. I was panting, and my eyes were filled with smarting tears. Then he turned around and walked back down the hall, leaving me standing there alone, a victim of my own raging emotions.

Also by Jennifer Wilde

MASTER OF PHOENIX HALL

WHEREVER LYNN GOES

Betrayal
at Blackcrest

JENNIFER WILDE
writing as Beatrice Parker

A DELL BOOK

Published by
Dell Publishing
a division of
Bantam Doubleday Dell Publishing Group, Inc.
666 Fifth Avenue
New York, New York 10103

ISBN: 0-440-20904-8

Printed in the United States of America

Published simultaneously in Canada

September 1991

10 9 8 7 6 5 4 3 2 1

RAD

I

I was lost. There was no denying it now. I had no earthly idea where I was. There had been a sign some miles back, but the rain had been falling so violently that I had been unable to read it properly. I was not really alarmed, not yet. I felt sure that this twisting back road would eventually take me to Hawkestown. The place had an improbable name, but the crumpled road map at my side assured me that it existed.

The rain fell in torrents, sweeping with small waves over the road ahead and splattering noisily over the windshield. I drove slowly. The tires slid over the wet pavement with a swishing sound, and the headlights barely penetrated the swirling sheets of rain. It seemed impossible that only a few hours ago I had been in London, closing up the flat in Chelsea and checking to see that the windows were locked and the gas properly shut off.

It was nice to be away for a while, even if I didn't know what to expect when I reached Hawkestown.

Getting away from the noise and furor of London for a week or so would do wonders for my morale. Perhaps when I returned my agent would have news of some wonderful job. That was just wishful thinking, I told myself, but I did not intend to worry. For at least a week I was going to devote myself to fun and relaxation. Perhaps Delia's new husband had a friend—male, unattached, and eager to meet a girl like me.

I pushed these thoughts out of my mind and concentrated on my driving. The inside of the car smelled of mothballs and dust. It rattled and chugged, but I had complete confidence in its ability to carry me safely to any given destination. I was not so sure about this particular destination. Had I made the right turnoff when I left the highway this afternoon? These country road markers were frightfully vague.

I had not passed a car in the last half-hour. For all purposes, the road belonged to me. It was narrow and in poor repair. Dark black trees grew close on either side, and their branches reached down like fingers to scratch the roof of the car. It was like driving through some ghostly tunnel. The clock on the dashboard informed me that it was after seven. It might be hours before I reached the house. I had no idea what Delia would think of my barging in on her in the middle of the night. Whatever her reactions, I could be sure they would be fraught with drama and completely typical.

I had a few things to say to Delia. None of them were flattering. I considered her neglect criminal. Even if she had given up a not quite glorious career to marry some country gentleman, that was no reason for not writing her only surviving relative. I had received no word from her since the enthusiastic and expensive telegram she had sent the day she arrived in Hawkestown.

That had been over a month ago. Since then there had not been even so much as a postcard. The promising young actress Delia Lane might now be the respectable Delia Hawke, chatelaine of a swell country estate and ever so elegant, but she need not think she could snub me. And if her mysterious new husband didn't approve of my unexpected visit, he could just lump it.

I intended to see Delia, and I intended to shake her by the shoulders. After that, of course, I would settle down and listen to all the delicious details of her new life. I could hardly wait to hear all about it. Knowing Delia, I was certain she had already managed to set the local gentry on their ears.

I swerved to avoid a rut in the road. The tires slid alarmingly. I clenched the steering wheel tightly and held my breath. The car righted itself and moved on down the road. The rain showed no signs of slacking. I would arrive at Blackcrest looking like a drowned sparrow. That would delight Delia, who always liked to have the upper hand. I would be in no state to meet the much discussed Derek Hawke. I was beginning to doubt the wisdom of my sudden trip.

I should have telephoned long distance to announce my arrival, but I had had no idea where to call. Delia had mentioned the house, Blackcrest, and had babbled merrily about its dark and bloody history, but I did not know where it was. I presumed it was somewhere near Hawkestown. For all I knew, Blackcrest might not even have telephones. From the way Delia described it, I would be surprised if it was even wired for electricity. I refused to speculate on the plumbing.

I knew so little about any of it. Delia, who was always so open and frank about all her affairs, had been deliberately evasive about everything concerning Mr. Derek Hawke. In the past, I had always met all her boyfriends, and she had been eager for my approval of them. Derek Hawke remained a man of mystery, although she kept promising to bring him to the flat to meet me. When she quit the show, drew her savings out of the bank, and left for Hawkestown, I had been quite dazed.

I could not believe that she was leaving. She had kissed me gaily on the cheek and assured me that everything was marvelous and we would see each other soon. Then she had gone, and the shabby little flat had seemed squalid and unbearable. We had shared it for years, ever since we had arrived in London, two orphaned teen-agers determined to find fame and fortune in the big city. Both assets had been highly elusive during the ensuing years.

Many people in our profession thought Delia and I were sisters. We were, in fact, first cousins, and Delia had lived with my family in Dorset ever since her own parents were killed in an automobile accident. We grew up together, inseparable companions, and when my own parents died, barely a month apart, Delia and I were left alone in the world. We spent little time grieving. We shook the dust of Dorset from our heels and left almost immediately for London.

We had many jobs, mostly menial, before either of us got a toehold in the theater. Delia landed in a revue and I finally got a series of walk-on parts with a repertory company. Delia soon soared with her raffish charm and incredible vivacity, and she had had steady if unspectacular employment ever since. My own climb had been more gradual and far less remunerative. Few people in England would recognize the name Deborah Lane, while almost everyone who attended music halls would remember Delia, though few could say what she had last appeared in.

When Delia left London I had been working as a guide in a museum, a "temporary" thing until my agent could find something more suitable. After a week, the museum job evaporated, too, and I had been living ever since on funds nervously withdrawn from my savings account. Deborah Lane had reached another of the all too frequent crossroads of her career and had decided to do something impulsive.

I had phoned my agent, closed the flat, taken my ancient car out of the garage, and headed for Hawkestown. Now, on this rainswept road, it seemed like sheer folly. Delia must have had her reasons for not writing, and I must have been out of my mind to have decided to call on her without the least warning. She would have every right to be furious. She might not even be home. She and her husband might still be on their honeymoon. I began to be plagued with doubts as the car hit a particularly nasty rut and skidded across the road.

The wheel seemed to jump out of my hand. The car shook and bounced viciously. I seized the wheel and managed to keep from going completely off the road. The car seemed to make a series of froglike leaps before lurching to a halt. The motor spluttered and the car sagged miserably in the rear. My heart sank as I realized what had happened. A tire had blown out. I was stranded in the middle of nowhere with a flat tire, in the midst of a downpour that would probably make history for its ferocity.

It was typical of my luck, I thought, and just what I needed to make the whole affair a total disaster.

I felt like bursting into tears. Instead, I let loose a series of highly descriptive words that were not ordinarily a part of my vocabulary. That relieved me somewhat, but the rain still poured on the roof of the car and I was nowhere nearer a solution to my dilemma.

I had a spare tire in the trunk and all the tools necessary to put it on. However, I was wearing my best white heels and a dress of white muslin printed with tiny pink and green flowers, my best, and I would starve to death before getting out in the rain thus attired. My luggage was in the trunk, too, so there could be no quick change in the front seat. I sat huddled over the steering wheel, listening to the rain and watching the minute hand of the clock slowly traverse the circle.

It was only a few minutes before the car passed, although it seemed like hours. It zoomed past, braked, then slowly reversed until it was directly in front of my own. I turned on my headlights in order to see better. The car was a jazzy red sports coupé, and the man climbing out of it was very tall, wearing a slick yellow mackintosh. I rolled down my window as he ambled over to the side of my car, for all the world as if this were a summer day without the least suggestion of rain.

"Trouble?" he inquired.

"Not a bit," I replied gaily. "I'm just admiring the scenery."

He missed the sarcasm. He pressed his brows together and looked at me as though I'd taken leave of my senses. The rain poured down on him. His hair fell in drenched dark curls over his forehead, and water ran in rivulets off his mackintosh. He seemed oblivious to it.

"I have a flat tire," I explained, somewhat impatiently.

"Oh?" He arched a brow.

"Jolly weather for it, isn't it?"

He seemed totally bewildered.

"You see," I said, "this dress cost a small fortune. I'm afraid I couldn't afford to ruin it. Consequently . . ."

"I'll change your tire for you," he said.

"You really are an angel," I replied, "but I couldn't ask you to do that."

I waited, tapping my fingers on the steering wheel. He was dreadfully slow in replying.

"Of course I will," he finally said. "Glad to be of assistance."

"My faith in mankind is restored," I said. "Here are the keys. If you will open the trunk, you'll find a somewhat bedraggled maroon suitcase. When you unfasten it, you'll find a long blue coat piled on top of some beige underwear. Ignore the underwear, but bring me the coat. I'll have to get out of the car while you're working."

"Good thinking," he said.

He brought me the coat promptly. I wrapped it around me and got out of the car. The shoes were ruined immediately, for I stepped into three inches of mud on the side of the road and almost lost my balance. My hair was drenched and hung in wet auburn clusters about my head. I huddled in the coat and shouted appropriate comments as the man in the yellow mackintosh jacked up the rear end of the car and removed the flat tire. He had pulled a flashlight out of his pocket and given it to me, directing me to hold it over the rear fender.

The light danced unsteadily over the area where he was working. The rain was falling so furiously that I could not hold it level. I dwelt on the ruined shoes, cursing myself for not leaving London in a sweater and a pair of slacks. Only an idiot would start off for a long drive in her best finery. It was just such thoughtlessness that made life so hazardous for a woman on her own.

The rain did not seem to bother the man. He rolled the spare into place and hoisted it up to fit on the metal rim. I marveled audibly at his agility and strength. He yelled back for me to keep the light away from the treetops and direct it on the car.

In a matter of minutes the job was done. He put the flat tire into the trunk and tossed the jack and wrench in after it. He slammed the lid down and stepped back. At that moment, ironically, the rain stopped. It ceased abruptly and completely. The sudden silence after the monotonous pounding was slightly unnerving. I stared at my savior.

"How's that for timing?" I remarked.

"Perfect," he replied.

He grinned. I was happy to see that he could take it all with some humor. It would have been maddening otherwise.

"Here are your keys," he said, handing them to me.

I returned his flashlight and smiled sincerely.

"I owe you quite a lot of thanks," I said soberly. "I

really don't know what I would have done if you hadn't come along."

"Ruined the dress, probably," he replied.

"Not on your life," I promised.

"Is everything all right now?" he asked. "Sure this thing will run properly?" He cast a disparaging glance at my battered old car.

"It may not look like much," I told him, "but it's a gem. I've depended on it for five years, and it's never let me down. Of course, the tires are another story. . . ."

"You'd better get in," he said. "It's quite cold, and you're wet. I would hate for you to catch cold."

I climbed back into the car and turned on the interior light in order to see better. The stranger in the mackintosh came over to the window and leaned his arms on the edge of it, his head level with mine. He smiled, quite amiable, and for the first time I realized what a vulnerable position I was in. This was an isolated spot, and there was no one else around. The man was a complete stranger. . . .

I relaxed. His dark brown eyes were very friendly, and I found it unthinkable that he could have ulterior motives. If he had been contemplating rape, I reasoned, he would never have changed my tire.

"Tell me," I said, "is there really a place called Hawkestown?"

"Without a doubt," he replied. "It's about two miles on down this road. You couldn't possibly miss it."

"I'm relieved," I said, wiping a damp lock from my temple. "I was beginning to think it was legendary— one of those places that appear only once every hundred years or so."

"It's real, all right," he said, "though few people have ever heard of it."

"I must admit I hadn't, until a relative of mine moved there. I am on my way to visit her now."

He was staring at me intently. His eyes were not merely looking at me, they were studying my features. I drew myself up, not at all sure that I liked this intense examination. The man noticed my concern, and he grinned.

"I don't suppose . . ." he began. "No, it couldn't be."

"I beg your pardon?"

"You're not by any chance Deborah Lane?"

"How on earth did you know?" I asked, startled.

"I've seen you on the screen."

His voice was low and hesitant, and I shook my head in disbelief. I could not believe that it was actually happening. After all this time, someone had actually recognized me. I felt like the celebrity I most assuredly was not. The stranger looked as though he were about to ask for my autograph. That would have been entirely too much for one night.

"I didn't know anyone actually saw that movie," I said.

"*The Sergeant's Secretary?* I saw it in Hawkestown. I never miss a J. Arthur Rank film. I don't know what to say. This is the first time I have ever met a movie star."

"Hardly that," I retorted. "It was my first and last film, and I had a very small part."

"It played in Hawkestown just a month ago. I saw it twice."

"They've released it in the provinces? I thought they were saving it to drop over enemy territory during the next war. The critics called it a 'Rank insult,' and that's the kindest thing they said about it."

"I enjoyed it," he protested.

"So did six other people," I replied blithely.

"How long will you be in Hawkestown?" he asked, changing the subject abruptly.

"Why—I have no idea," I stammered. "Why?"

"Well, I did go to a lot of trouble to change your tire. I feel I should have some kind of reward, don't you? How about having dinner with me tomorrow night?"

"I don't even know your name," I said.

"Alex Tanner," he replied, "short for Alexander."

The name was vaguely familiar. I felt I should recognize it, but my memory drew a total blank. Mr. Tanner was strongly attractive with his crooked nose and large mouth and those magnetic brown eyes, although he could by no means be called handsome. The prospect of having dinner with him was thoroughly pleasant.

"Aren't you rushing things a bit, Mr. Tanner?" I asked.

"Not at all. I merely want to tell all my friends I've had dinner with a film star. It'll give me ever so much status in Hawkestown. You can't refuse, you know. I *did* fix your flat. . . ."

"I'm not at all sure I can make it," I said.

"Sure you can. There's not that much to do in Hawkestown."

"My cousin may have plans. . . ."

Alex Tanner shrugged his shoulders. He twisted his large mouth into a most fascinating grin, and I knew it was hopeless. I had never been able to resist boyish charm combined with rugged masculinity, and Alex Tanner possessed both characteristics in abundance.

"Look," he said, "you can't disappoint a fan."

"Well—" I deliberated.

"I'll be at the Sable tomorrow night at eight. It's the only restaurant in Hawkestown. I'll be sitting at a table for two, waiting, and I'll expect you to be there on the dot."

"You take a lot for granted," I said.

He nodded in agreement and flashed that grin again. I turned the key in the ignition and gunned the motor. He told me that he would follow me to Hawkestown to see that I had no more trouble, and then he got into his own car and pulled up so that I could pass. He raised his arm in a little salute as I pulled around him.

The road ahead was like a dark black ribbon, gleaming with wet. I drove faster now, and in my rear-view mirror I could see his headlights close behind. I felt safe and secure, and there was a warm glow that I had not felt in too long a time. I drove into the outskirts of Hawkestown and slowed. Alex Tanner zoomed past me, the jazzy red sports coupé speeding on down the road at a frightful speed. I smiled to myself. I had almost forgotten about Delia and her mysterious new husband.

2

Hawkestown was a tiny place, what businesses there were centered around a little square in the center of town. Behind these were some impressive-looking homes and, farther away, several neat cottages sheltered by huge oak trees. The oak trees grew everywhere, and in summer Hawkestown would be shady and cool. A capricious river wound through the town, and the road passed over several stone bridges. Although it was not yet nine, the town seemed shut down and asleep, with only a few squares of yellow light showing through the windows. I had an impression of a place lost to time, untouched by the frantic modern pace of today. It was the kind of town one would love to visit for two weeks of rest. During the third week claustrophobia would set in.

I was sure it had enormous charm by day, with its gardens and rustic buildings, but now it was all black and gray, gilded with moonlight. I could see the dark shapes of trees and the glittering silver ribbon of river that twisted and turned through the town. I drove past the square and saw the tarnished bronze statue of a man on horseback that stood directly in the middle of it, several farm wagons pulled up around it. I saw the post office and bank, a drugstore, and the cinema where Alex Tanner had witnessed the Rank disaster. I passed a few large private homes set behind picket fences, and then the road wound through a wooded area. My gas tank showed empty, while my stomach growled in protest of its recent lack of sustenance. I was beginning to despair of filling either.

Hawkestown certainly had little to offer the weary traveler. It was completely off the beaten track, far away from any of the modern highway arteries, and quite obviously, no tourist attraction. I wondered if any place was open. I had to get directions to Blackcrest, and if possible, phone to announce my arrival. The motor began to jerk and sputter, and the gas-gauge needle danced maddeningly about the *E*. I visualized myself stranded again, with no handsome Alex around to help. I gnawed my lower lip nervously. Then I saw the lights ahead.

The place was low and flat, standing in the middle of an expanse of crushed-white-shell pavement, and garishly colored lights spilled out of every window. A bright ruby-red neon sign flashed on and off, promising FOOD, and three pale blue petrol pumps stood before the wooden canopy in front of the main entrance. Several cars were parked at the side of the building. Even as I pulled up in front of one of the pumps I could hear pop music blaring loudly.

It was a heavenly sight, however incongruous with the rest of the neighborhood. Even Hawkestown, I surmised, couldn't completely escape the twentieth century. A boy came out of the building to assist me, and he suited the mood of the place ideally. He wore too-tight black pants, a black leather jacket that was too shiny, and a sullen scowl that went with the outfit. His dark blond hair was worn too long, in the fashion of current London youth, and he had all the earmarks of the rude, rowdy young men who seemed to delight in making nuisances of themselves before going up to Oxford and, ultimately, becoming the backbone of the nation. I smiled tolerantly as he swaggered over to the car and twisted his lips into a sneer that many would have considered threatening.

"Yeah?" he muttered.

"Do you sell petrol?" I asked.

"These pumps ain't for ornament," he growled.

I blinked at the grammar and looked up at him with eyes that I hoped were very blue and innocent. The boy stood beside the car with his hands jammed in his pockets, his head cocked a little to one side. His eyes were dark brown, glowing, surrounded by long curling lashes that somewhat lessened their animal ferocity. The eyes were a startling contrast to the thick blond hair, and ferocious expression notwithstanding, the boy was unusually attractive. He was tall, with a muscular build, and he had that red-blooded glow of the very young that no amount of posturing could disguise.

"You want petrol, lady?" he said, impatient.

"If you could see your way clear—" I began.

"Shall I fill 'er up?"

"Please do," I replied, very gracious. "Is there a place where I could freshen up a bit?"

He jerked his head, indicating a walk that wound around behind the building. I assumed it led to the

rest rooms. I got out of the car and took a small over-
night case out of the trunk. The boy was pulling a
hose over to the gas tank, and he ignored me completely as I walked past him and around the pale blue
pumps.

The rest room was small but well lighted, all done
in green tiles. There was a large mirror hanging over
the sink, and I blanched when I finally got around to
looking in it. No cinema star ever looked so pale and
frightening. I was frankly surprised that Alex Tanner
hadn't turned and run. My makeup had worn off and
my hair hung in limp, damp ringlets about a face I
liked to think classical in shape. I took my hairbrush
out of the case and attacked the hair. After a while it
began to take on some of the shape and texture I was
ordinarily so proud of. I wore it long and it fell in
natural waves of russet shade with deep copper highlights. I put the brush aside and tossed my head, satisfied with the way the locks fell.

It took me a little longer to apply the makeup. I
wanted to look my best when I confronted Delia and
her husband. I worked diligently, finally stepping
back to survey the results. They were pleasing. The
face that had impressed Alex Tanner so much when
he saw it on the screen would never be beautiful in
the traditional sense, but I liked to tell myself that
character and bone structure were more important. I
had high cheekbones, a straight nose, and full lips
that were a little too wide. My eyes were large, set
wide apart, deep blue with a hint of green. The lashes
were long and curling and the brows made perfect
cinnamon-colored arches over lids that were shadowed ever so slightly with jade.

The face would never launch a thousand ships, but

in its time it had graced several dozen beer advertisements with profitable and unexpected results. The movie director had seen my face on a billboard, and finding that I was tall and slender as well as photogenic, had hired me for the small part in his film. History was not made, but my bank account was fattened considerably.

I had brought a pair of shabby pink low-heeled shoes in the case. I removed the ruined white heels, unceremoniously and regretfully dumped them in the garbage bin, and put on the clean ones. I felt much better, ready now to face anything.

I went inside the building. The first thing I saw was a jukebox. It was also the first thing I heard. A rock group were yelling about an unrequited love affair, and as the record spun two teen-age girls sitting at the counter snapped their fingers and shook their shoulders with the music. There were several dark booths along one wall, and I sat at one of them, contemplating the delights of hamburger, french fries, and hot coffee. When I saw the plate of food the waitress set before one of the girls, I decided to settle for coffee.

The waitress took my order, and I looked around at the hot spot of Hawkestown. It obviously catered to teen-agers, for I was the only adult in evidence. A group of youngsters huddled at one of the booths, while another group surrounded the jukebox, ready to drop in more coins just as soon as the final scream of the current record threatened a moment of silence. The girls all wore miniskirts or slacks suits, rainbow-colored. The boys were dressed in attire similar to that of the young gallant who had waited on me outside.

He came in through the front door. The girls sitting

at the counter giggled and nudged one another. I heard one of them call him Neil. Neil was very aware of the attention focused on him. He ran his brown fingers through the shaggy blond hair and curled his lips as he moved past the girls on his way to speak to the waitress. As he spoke to the woman, he glared at the girls with hostile brown eyes. His disdain was obvious, even to them. They both squirmed and seemed to adore him even more.

Knighthood is no longer in flower, I said to myself as I stirred my coffee.

I noticed a telephone booth in one corner, and I was about to make inquiries about Blackcrest when the front door opened and a young girl came in. She was so breathtakingly lovely that I paused, openly staring at her.

She was painfully young, surely not more than seventeen, and she moved across the room with all the grace and hesitancy of a young doe. I had never seen such grace of movement, so fluid and natural that it approached artistry. Her hair was platinum, with that glossy sheen that can never come from a bottle, pinned up on her head in lustrous waves. Her features were delicate, fragile, the enormous eyes gentian blue, the lips as pink and perfectly shaped as a rosebud. She wore a white raincoat belted at the waist, and she looked as out of place in this motley assortment of youngsters as a fairy child among gremlins.

She moved over to the counter where Neil was standing. Everyone in the place stared at her, but she did not seem to notice. Her eyes were on the boy behind the counter, and the place might have been empty except for him. Neil shifted uneasily, glancing around distastefully as the girl approached. The girl whispered something to him, and he shot her a warning look that clearly told her to be careful what she said.

The girl stepped back. Her incredible blue eyes looked as if they might dissolve with tears. She stood with her shoulders hunched up, as though expecting a blow. I had never seen anything so touching in my life. The boy jerked his head, indicating that she should go back outside, and she left the room as silently and gracefully as she had come in. I watched the door swing to behind her, and I was moved by the episode, which seemed as tragic and poignant as anything I had ever seen in the theater.

I slid out of the booth and walked over to the counter.

"Could you tell me where I could find the home of Derek Hawke?" I asked the waitress.

She arched an eyebrow and gave me a look that could only be called incredulous. The boy called Neil was standing nearby, and the waitress turned to him as though expecting some special instruction. Neil gave a quick glance at the door that had just closed on the girl; then he moved along behind the counter until he was standing beside the waitress. They both stared at me.

"I believe it's called Blackcrest," I said, puzzled.

"Everyone knows where Blackcrest is," the boy said.

"Few people ask how to get there, though," the waitress added.

"You intend to go there?" the boy asked rudely.

"Of course not," the waitress said. "She merely wants to know where it is."

I felt like asking if they were in vaudeville. I tapped my foot impatiently.

"Is the number in the phone book?" I asked.

"Phone lines blew down in the rainstorm," the waitress said. "The crew're workin' on them now, but they won't be back up for hours. Besides, it's an unlisted number."

"Swell," I said. "You've been a great help."

The waitress blinked dumbly, and the boy continued to stare at me. His look was not hostile now. It was wary. He seemed to be examining me for defects. I felt my cheeks flush with irritation. I had asked a relatively simple question. Judging from the reactions to it, I might have inquired where the body was buried. After a moment the boy lowered his eyes and spoke in a voice that was both polite and somber.

"Blackcrest is about a mile on down the road," the boy said. "You drive on the way you're headed, and you come to a bridge. Beyond that, you'll see a turn-off between two stone pillars. You turn there. It's a private drive."

"Thank you," I replied icily.

The boy moved away, and I settled the bill for the petrol and coffee with the waitress. She was a plump creature with a bovine pink face. A pair of golden earrings dangled from her earlobes, and her jaws moved around a wad of gum. She stared at me with frank curiosity as she took my money and returned the change.

"Not many people go to Blackcrest," she remarked as I dropped the coins in my purse.

"Oh?"

"The Hawke don't like havin' people around."

"The Hawke? You mean Mr. Derek Hawke?"

"The same. He don't like havin' people hangin' around. He don't like people, period."

I snapped my purse shut and regarded her with lifted brow.

"I'm sure he'll just adore me," I remarked caustically. "I know all sorts of tricks."

The waitress blinked again, and I swept out of the room, almost colliding with a girl in purple slacks and a long-haired lad with a guitar slung over his shoulder. I closed the door behind me, glad to shut off some of the din. For some reason or other, the ruby-red neon with its fraudulent promise was no longer flashing, and it was relatively dark as I walked around the pumps to my car.

The air was cool and fresh, doubly welcome after the odors inside. I stood with my hand on the door handle, breathing deeply. The moon was behind a bank of clouds, and as I watched, it broke loose from its concealment and poured silver light from the heavens. I looked at the sky, a gray velvet expanse filled with ponderous black clouds. Silver spilled from the ragged edges of the clouds. There was a milky glow in the air, and everything below was picked out in shades of black and gray, silver, and dark blue.

I started to open the car door when I heard the voices. They were quite near, and at first I was startled. They were coming from the side of the building. From where I stood I could barely see two shapes leaning against the wall there.

"It's out of the question, Honora. We'll have to wait."

"I've been waiting for over a year. I can't wait any longer."

"You'll have to."

"I won't!" The voice was desperate. "I'll leave without you. You don't care anyway. You'd like for me to do that. Then you'd be free of me. You wouldn't have to worry—"

"Shut up!"

A ray of moonlight illuminated the spot where they stood. The girl in the white raincoat was leaning against the wall, flattened against it as though for protection. Most of her body was hidden by the boy who stood directly in front of her, his palms resting along the wall beside her arms, his body hovering over hers. His legs were planted wide apart, and his broad shoulders encased in shiny black leather hid her face.

"You shouldn't have come here," he said. His voice was angry. He might have been admonishing a disobedient child. "If they found out—"

"I don't care," she protested. "I want them to know. I want everyone to know. I have a right—"

"Not for a few months you don't," he retorted. "If you're not careful—"

"You don't care anything about me," she said, and her voice was suddenly calm. "It isn't me you're interested in, is it? That's what he says. It's the money. That's the only reason—"

Her voice stopped abruptly, as though a hand had been clamped over it, or a pair of lips. I climbed into the car and started the motor. I felt guilty for having eavesdropped for as long as I had. The boy had evidently wanted privacy or he would not have switched off the neon. My insatiable curiosity about other people had forced me to linger there a moment, listening. The constant cavalcade of drama in the life around me never failed to intrigue. There was romance and excitement even in such a forgotten place as Hawkes-town, it seemed.

Beyond the fuel station and café, the road wound through more wooded area. The headlights made dim yellow spears that cut across the dark black trunks of trees. The road was narrow and poorly paved, full of ruts and holes. Water stood in low places, splashing loudly as I passed over them. I was still worried about the tires. Another blowout would be disastrous now. This road made the other look like a superhighway, and I was certain no one would come zooming past in a sports car. I gave a little sigh of relief as I passed over the stone bridge. A bit farther down the road I saw the two towering stone pillars and turned off on the road between them.

If it was a private road, it was certainly kept up better than the public one. The tires purred over the smooth expanse. The road twisted and turned with an alarming number of curves, and huge trees grew close on either side. I wondered if it would never end. I went around another curve, fully expecting to see the house, but there was only more road. I had begun to think the boy had sent me on a wild-goose chase, but then I passed through two more stone pillars, smaller than the others. The trees fell away, to be replaced by evergreens and formal shrubs. The road ended, and I was on a great crushed-shell drive. I held my breath. Blackcrest stood before me in all its towering majesty.

3

I had never seen anything so immense and formidable. Delia had described the house to me from a picture her future husband had shown her, but the description had prepared me for nothing like this. The main section of the house was three stories high. On both sides of it a wing branched off, winding around to the back, where a tower jutted up over the roofs. Part of the tower had crumbled away, but it still reared up in Gothic splendor. Washed now with moonlight, the dark blue slate roofs gleamed silver, the chimneys and turrets and abutments casting long black shadows. Blackcrest was constructed of heavy blocks of dark gray stone with all the tortured carvings and corners of an era long since vanished. The windows were like flat black eyes staring down at me. Tendrils of dark green ivy covered half of the front, the leaves rattling like sheets of metal in the wind.

I parked the car in front of the immense black marble portico, marveling at the impressive ugliness of a mansion that had been standing for over two hundred years. The place was intimidating. It seemed to be watching me, waiting to swallow me up. It had an aura of evil and age that was almost tangible, and I was irritated to find my shoulders trembling slightly as I moved up the steps under the portico. The porch was a nest of shadows. Drafts of cold air blew my hair. The door was black oak, polished smooth with age, and in dead center of it a brass knocker shaped like a hawk hung heavily on a brass ring. The brass was icy when I touched it. I pounded on the door, trying not to think of the stories of Edgar Allan Poe I had once read so avidly.

I could hear the noise of the knocker echoing in the hall beyond the door, and when I stopped knocking the silence was heavy, as though someone just inside stood poised, listening. I found it impossible to believe that anyone as bright and vivacious as Delia could actually live in such a place. I lifted the heavy knocker again, pounding it against the wood. Still no one came. I would have returned to the car, but for some strange reason I was afraid to turn my back on the house.

I chided myself. The house was large, and it was old. In the moonlight it had an undeniably eerie atmosphere, but that was no reason to let my imagination run wild. It was very late, and no one was expecting me. The servants probably slept in the back part of the house and everyone else was probably upstairs asleep. I pounded again, determined to get some answer. I still could not shake the feeling that someone stood just beyond the door, listening to me.

Five minutes had passed, perhaps more. I had seen no lights burning in any of the windows, but I was certain someone was at home. Even if Delia and her husband were not here, they would hardly have left the house vacant. There must be a servant, a caretaker, someone who would tell me where my cousin was.

I backed away from the door. I was frightened, even though I told myself it was an absurd sensation. Something was wrong. My instincts warned me to flee quickly, even if it meant another long drive back to Blackcrest in the light of day. I was contemplating this when a light came on and illuminated the porch with a dim yellow glow. At the same moment, the great door swung inward.

A man stood in the doorway. The light was burning in the hall behind him, and he stood in silhouette. He was very tall and thin, but I could not see his features clearly until he stepped onto the porch. He was very old, his hair silver, his face wrinkled. His cold blue eyes regarded me with an icy stare. He wore a black uniform, obviously hastily pulled on. The jacket hung loosely, not properly buttoned.

"Yes?" he inquired. His ancient voice was as hard as granite.

"I'm Deborah Lane," I said, as though that explained everything.

He arched an eyebrow and continued to regard me with that disdainful expression.

"Yes?" he repeated.

"I've come to see Mrs. Hawke," I explained.

"Mrs. Hawke does not receive visitors at this hour," he said.

I drew myself up with what I hoped was an imperious manner. I might be calling at an inconvenient hour, but I was not about to be snubbed by a mere servant. I glared at him with eyes as icy as his own. When I spoke, my voice would have done justice to any peeress extant.

"I'm quite sure she will see me," I informed him.

"I'm afraid I can't allow that," he replied.

"But—I'm her cousin," I protested, losing my nerve. The man shook his head slowly, his icy blue eyes never leaving my own. I gnawed my lower lip nervously, finding it hard to keep tears of frustration out of my eyes.

"Mrs. Hawke has no cousin," he said.

"But she does," I exclaimed. "I haven't heard from her in over a month, and I've come all this way—"

"What is it, Morris?"

The voice came from somewhere beyond the door, and it was a husky, guttural voice. The servant turned around, but not before I saw the expression of alarm on his face. His regal manner vanished, and he looked nervous. His fingers flew to his jacket, fastening it properly. He was quite obviously terrified of his employer.

"A young lady, sir," he said, speaking to someone I could not see. He darted a quick look at me, as though wishing I would vanish, and then he drew himself up as his employer approached.

"Show her in, Morris," the man said firmly.

"This way, miss," Morris said, holding the door for me.

I stepped inside, gripping my shabby leather suitcase. I found myself in an immense hall with brown and maroon wallpaper over dark mahogany wainscoting. At one end of it a spiral staircase curved up into the shadows, and directly over my head a chandelier with tarnished crystal pendants poured feeble light over the worn maroon carpet.

"That will be all, Morris," the stranger said.

The old servant shuffled away down the hall. I was alone with the master of Blackcrest. I set down my suitcase and sighed with relief. I smiled at Derek Hawke, but there was no welcoming smile in return. He stood with his hands in the pockets of his robe, looking at me with obvious mistrust. He looked as though he expected me to pull a gun and demand the family silver.

"You must be Derek," I said with a charming lilt.

"I am Derek Hawke, yes."

"I'm Deborah Lane. Delia must have told you all about me."

He made no reply. He still regarded me with wary eyes. I felt that Delia had done well for herself. Derek Hawke was quite clearly a man of affluence, and though by no means handsome, he emanated an animal magnetism that was overwhelming.

He was extremely tall, over six feet, and lean, with a sharp, lanky body that had all the grace and power of a panther's. His features were strong and angular, the cheekbones high and bony, the nose twisted a little to one side, the lips large and wide, out of proportion with the rest of the face. His eyes were brown, so dark that they looked black, glowering beneath heavy, hooded lids. Dark black brows arched over the lids, and thick waves of raven-black hair spilled untidily over his tan forehead.

He stood with his broad, bony shoulders hunched forward, his hands hidden in the pockets of a black brocade robe embroidered with thread of darker black silk. He must have been in his middle thirties, a formidable man who would understandably strike terror in the hearts of simpleminded people like the waitress. I could visualize him wearing the robes of the Inquisition, or in pirate boots and saber, but I could certainly not see him in a parlor in Mayfair.

"Where is Delia?" I asked, looking around as though expecting her to come rushing toward me.

"Delia?" he said.

"My cousin. Your wife . . ."

"I'm afraid there has been some mistake," he said calmly.

I smiled again. "I know this is unexpected, but you will forgive me, won't you? I didn't have an address, so I couldn't write, and when I arrived in Hawkestown I found the telephone wires had blown down. You can understand my dilemma. Delia hasn't written or phoned since the wedding, and I'm out of work now and had nothing to do, so, on impulse, decided to pay an impromptu visit. . . ."

I had been talking rapidly, nervously, smiling as I chattered on, and Derek Hawke had not moved a muscle in his face. The dark, glowering eyes never left my face. The large, wide lips were held in a rigid line of disapproval. I cut myself short and looked at him, afraid now. Something was wrong. I had sensed it immediately.

"I don't know what your game is, young woman," the man said, "but I can assure you you won't get far with it here. I don't like intruders at Blackcrest, particularly intruders who claim I'm married to a woman I've never heard of in my life."

I stared at him in stunned silence. Then I gave a nervous laugh.

"We'll exchange jokes in the morning," I said.

"Right now I would like to see Delia. Will you fetch her?"

"Perhaps you didn't understand me," Derek Hawke replied stiffly.

"But—" I began. "You're Derek Hawke. This is Blackcrest. Delia told me—"

"I've never heard of this woman," he said.

"She's your wife. The butler said Mrs. Hawke—"

"The Mrs. Hawke that Morris referred to is my aunt. She is sixty years old."

The words did not seem to register. I stared at him for a long time with eyes that did not seem to focus properly. My hands seemed to move of their own accord, fumbling with my purse and taking out the crumpled telegram she had sent me. I held it out, and at the same moment my legs seemed to give way.

My face was buried among the folds of black silk. Strong arms supported me. I tried to raise my head, but it seemed to take far more effort than I could muster. The next thing I knew I was being guided into another room, the ironlike arms holding me, the wiry body forcing me to move. Derek Hawke led me to a sofa, forced me down to the cushions. When, moments later, I sat up, the mists evaporating from my brain, he was standing over me, a glass of brandy in his hand.

"Drink this," he ordered.

"I never drink," I said.

"Drink it," he commanded.

I took the glass with trembling hand. I drank the fiery liquid. It burned fiercely, but it enabled me to see clearly. I put the glass down on the table beside the sofa and looked up at the man who hovered over me.

"I never faint either," I said, knowing how foolish it sounded.

"Then that was quite an effective act, Miss Lane."

"It wasn't an act," I replied.

"You're sure? This whole thing seems to be one great act to me. I want to know what you think you're up to?"

"I think you'd better let me ask the questions, Mr. Hawke," I said. My voice quivered, and it distressed me.

I sat up straight and pulled my skirt over my knees. I was so weak I did not think I could manage to stand for a while yet. Derek Hawke was looking down at me with hooded lids, his arms folded across his chest. I had to tilt my head back to meet his gaze. It was no position from which to be grand, yet I managed to sound as though I were in full command of the situation when I spoke again.

"What have you done with Delia?" I asked. My voice was hard, and it carried beautifully.

"Nothing at all."

"Where is she?"

"I have no idea."

"What have you *done* with her?" I repeated.

"My dear young woman, I will tell you one more time. I have never seen this woman you refer to."

"You have the telegram. Read it."

"I have already done so."

"Are you still going to tell me—"

"I am going to tell you nothing," he said.

He strolled across the room and took a slender brown cigar out of a box that sat on the mantel. He rolled the cigar between his fingers before putting it in his mouth. He struck a match, cupping his hands over the flame and raising it to the cigar. Then he stood at the hearth, one arm resting along the mantel. His dark eyes watched me, and he seemed to be contemplating the best way to dispose of me. The butt of the cigar glowed as he pulled on it. He removed it and blew a cloud of smoke. His lids narrowed.

"I must warn you that I've had plenty of experience with blackmailers," he said. "A man in my position frequently has to deal with such people. The fact that you are young and attractive will not make me any more lenient if you persist in this charade."

"You think I've come to blackmail you?"

"What else should I think?"

"I don't know, Mr. Hawke."

I was calm now, in complete possession of myself. Derek Hawke was undoubtedly shrewd, but I could see through his accusations. He wanted to put me on the defensive. It would give him more time, and he needed time to formulate some story. I did not know what he had done with Delia, but I did know that he had not reckoned on my coming here like this and confronting him. It had taken him by surprise, and he was trying to cover up by attacking me before I could voice my own accusations.

"Delia is not at Blackcrest?" I said.

"Certainly not."

"She has never been here?"

He shook his head slowly.

"I don't believe you," I said.

"If you searched the place, you would find no sign of her, nor any sign that she had ever been here."

He swept his arm out, as though bidding me to make such a search. It was an elegant gesture. There was nothing of the dandy about Derek Hawke, yet he was an aristocrat, hard, cruel, elegant in every respect. His voice, so harsh, so reminiscent of movie gangsters in smoke-filled dives, only emphasized this refined, steellike elegance. It was not simulated. He had the same natural quality that made the lion superior to other beasts, and it was real, an almost tangible part of him. He was born to dictate, to rule, and he would allow nothing to jeopardize this right.

I knew I was up against something far too strong, but I was not going to give way. I intended to fight him, however impossible that might seem at the moment.

"She told me she met you in London," I said.

"Then she was lying."

"She described you. She described this house."

"With a little research, anyone could do that."

"The telegram—"

"It's real, no doubt, but it contains lies."

"I believe you're the one who is lying."

"Do you, Miss Lane?"

"I think the police would be interested in this, Mr. Hawke."

"I'm sure they would be. However, it might prove embarrassing for you."

"What do you mean?"

"I mean that I am not Bluebeard, nor do I run a white-slavery ring during my spare time. I've never seen this woman, nor has she ever been inside my home. I can prove that, and if you insist on continuing with this farce, I'm sure my lawyers can find some way of restraining you."

"You can't intimidate me," I said.

"No?"

"I'm not afraid of you—or your lawyers."

"You don't give up easily, do you, Miss Lane?"

"Not at all," I replied.

"Rest assured I was making no idle threat. The police would laugh at your story, and my lawyers would see to it that you paid the penalty for such accusations against me. There are libel laws, Miss Lane."

I stared at him. I could think of nothing to say. My chin trembled and I was afraid I was going to burst into tears. That would have been disastrous. I glanced about the dimly lit room, taking in details I had not noticed before. I saw the dark walls with the faded tapestries hanging on them, the ancient chairs covered with worn green velvet, the tables carved of some dark, heavy wood. My eyes kept returning to the man who stood so menacingly at the hearth, smoking the cigar. He would be capable of anything, I thought, anything at all.

I contained my alarm. It would do no good for me to give in to the emotions that seemed to be bursting inside. Delia was missing. This man knew where she was, or what had happened to her. At the moment he was the only avenue to her. Whatever he had done, he had not been careless about it; of that I was certain. If he said he could prove she had never been here, he could. I felt cold all over as I watched him crush out the cigar and move slowly toward me.

"Hasn't this gone far enough?" he asked. There was a note of kindness in his guttural voice, and for a moment I almost believed he had been telling the truth. "Surely you realize you can't carry this thing through? I don't know what you were intending to do, but it won't work. I can assure you of that."

I stood up. I met his gaze with level eyes.

"I'm sorry to have troubled you, Mr. Hawke," I said.

"No trouble. It's been most interesting."

He seemed to be relaxed now, ready to pass the whole thing off. He was very convincing. Had Delia not talked about him for a month before she left London, had she not described him and the house with such perfect detail, and had I not received the telegram from Hawkestown, I would have found it easy to believe everything he said. As it was, I knew he was lying, and I intended to stay in Hawkestown until I found out exactly what had happened to my cousin.

"I've met many confidence men in my life," he said, "but never one so attractive. Try someone more gullible next time, Miss Lane. You've stepped out of your league with me."

Don't bet on it, I said to myself.

"May I have the telegram back, Mr. Hawke?"

"Oh no, Miss Lane. I'll keep that." He patted his pocket. "It'll be interesting to trace it."

He gave me a tight smile. It would prove useless to argue with him, and I was certainly not strong enough to take it from him by force. The telegram was the only tangible evidence I had, and now Derek Hawke had taken it. I might not have the slip of paper, but the words on it were engraved in my memory. He couldn't take that.

"I must go," I said, gathering up my purse.

"Not just yet," he replied.

"It's very late."

"Far too late for you to be out alone." Derek Hawke said. "It's a long drive back to Hawkestown, and you'd never find a room at this time of night. You'd better stay here till morning."

"I wouldn't dream of it."

I started as a clap of thunder crashed outside. A flash of lightning followed, and the lights of the chandelier flickered a moment before maintaining their dim glow. Rain began to fall again. I could hear it pattering loudly on the terrace outside.

"That settles it," he remarked. "You'll stay."

"I'm afraid not," I replied firmly. I started toward the door, but Derek Hawke reached it before I did. He stood in the doorway, leaning against the frame and barring the way.

"Please move," I said.

"I can't let you leave," he replied. "Suppose something happened? The roads are terrible. It's raining. If you had an accident, it would be on my conscience. It's better that you stay."

"Mr. Hawke—"

"Be reasonable, Miss Lane."

He did not intend to let me leave. He intended for me to stay here so that there would be no immediate danger of my going to the police. He would have time during the night to work things out, to see that there were no loose ends he had failed to cover up. Perhaps he even thought he could still convince me I was mistaken about him. At any rate, he had no intentions of letting me leave Blackcrest with things in their present state.

"Several people know I've come here," I lied.

"Do they, indeed?"

"And I stopped at a café in Hawkestown. I asked directions to get to Blackcrest."

"Did you?"

"I think you'd better let me pass."

Derek Hawke smiled at me. The wide lips curled at

the corners, and his eyes sparkled momentarily with amusement. He gave a short, harsh little laugh.

"Do you think I intend to murder you during the night? Really, Miss Lane, isn't that a bit melodramatic? Surely even you can see the absurdity of it."

"I didn't say I thought that."

"Nevertheless, you thought you'd take precautions." I glared at him. My cheeks were flushed.

"I don't think I should stay," I said, as calmly as possible.

"I insist," he said smoothly. "I wouldn't send anyone out on a night like this. You'll stay the night, Miss Lane. One thing Blackcrest has is plenty of room. Perhaps in the morning we can discuss this further and reach some amiable conclusions."

He spoke the words with the firm, friendly insistence of the determined host. I did not protest any further. It suited my purposes to remain here. I was in no danger, and I would have an opportunity to find out more about the man. I stepped back, resigned.

"I'll ring for Morris," he said. "He will show you upstairs to one of the guest rooms. It isn't often I have an opportunity to display hospitality at Blackcrest. Don't deny me that chance now."

I made no reply. I watched him as he stepped over to the wall and tugged a silken cord. I could hear a bell ringing somewhere in the back regions of the house. Derek Hawke turned to me and smiled. It was going to be cat and mouse, I reflected, but it would behoove anyone to know which was the cat, which the mouse.

4

The sound of the rain pounding on the roof was steady and monotonous. It finally lulled me to sleep. I had lain awake for what seemed like hours, my brain whirling with questions. Delia's bright, pert face seemed to float before me, and then the dark eyes of Derek Hawke stared from out of the darkness, his wide lips twisting into a smile. The bed was warm, the feather pillow soft, and layers of unconsciousness superimposed one another until I floated in a dark void where nebulous gray shapes moved slowly against a darker gray field. Once I thought I heard angry voices outside the room, but I thought it must have been part of a dream.

The room was filled with misty gray light when I opened my eyelids. Through the window I could see streaks of pinkish orange. I was drowsy, and for a moment I could not remember where I was. Some sound had awakened me. The sound was repeated. Someone was opening the door, and the hinges creaked slightly. I lowered my lashes, peering through them as a shadowy form moved slowly into the room.

It was the girl I had seen last night when I stopped for petrol. I thought I must still be dreaming. She slipped across the room and stood over the bed, peering down at me with those enormous blue eyes. She wore a pale blue nightgown, and her silvery hair was fastened loosely with a blue ribbon. She was there only a moment, her pink lips slightly parted as though she wanted to whisper something, and then she was gone. There was no sound as the door closed behind her.

I sighed, turning my head into the soft folds of the pillow. When I finally woke up, the room was flooded with sunlight, and a bird warbled lustily outside my window. I sat up, shaking away the last vestiges of sleep. I tried to remember the dream, not at all sure the girl had not really been here. I heard voices in the hallway outside my door.

"Are you going to wake her up?"

"It's late, Miss Honora. The master wants her to join him in the breakfast room."

"She was sleeping so soundly when I saw her."

"He'd be furious if he knew you'd slipped in to see her. He's already in a rage after what you done last night. Has a right to be, too, if you ask me. Sneakin' off like that an' then comin' in all wet in the middle of the night—"

"It's none of your business, Betty."

"That it ain't, to be sure. But I'd be careful, just the same. When he finds out who it is you're sneakin' off to see—"

"How do you know who it is?"

"I'm sure it ain't no secret among the help, missy."

"Do you intend to tell him?"

"I believe in mindin' my own business, and that's a fact. Run along now, Miss Honora. Stay out of the way and behave yourself."

"I must speak to the woman—"

"You'll have your chance later on, missy. Now scoot. The master is waitin' for her now, and he's gettin' impatient. I'm sure I don't know what things are comin' to—strangers comin' in and stayin' the night, an' people yellin' at each other in the small hours so's a person can't get a wink of sleep—"

The door flew open and a plump woman in her late thirties came into the room, marching briskly over to the window and jerking the draperies all the way open. The sunlight, brilliant before, was blinding now, and I groaned, throwing one arm out in protest. This seemed to delight the maid. A pert little smile played at the corners of her pink lips. There was a merry twinkle in her bright blue eyes. Short, rotund, with fiery red curls now frosted with gray, she had the cozy yet determined manner of the maid who has been with the family for years and regards the house and everything in it as her own private property. She wore a neat blue uniform and a starched white apron. A whimsical white cap perched atop the short red curls.

"Did you have to do that?" I asked irritably.

"A person needs sunlight," she replied primly.

"Not that much," I protested, "and not this early."

She told me in no uncertain terms that it was after ten o'clock and regarded me with a look that plainly expressed her opinion of anyone who could still be in bed at such an hour. I felt completely immoral under the surveillance of those eyes. Betty was a brisk, efficient person who would clearly stand for no nonsense, I reflected, and yet I liked her immensely on sight. She reminded me of a maid we had had in Dorset years ago.

"I'm Betty, ma'am," she said. "I've come to tell you that the master wishes to see you. He's waitin' in the breakfast room. When you're ready to come down, I'll show you the way."

"Thank you, Betty," I said in a very friendly voice. "How is Mrs. Hawke this morning?"

"I'm sure I wouldn't know. She's still with her cats. You wouldn't catch me anywhere *near* those wretched beasts."

"Cats?"

"Cats. The old lady collects 'em. A cat hasn't been drowned in the county for fifteen years. People just bring 'em to the gates and turn 'em loose. They know the old lady'll take 'em in and coddle 'em and give 'em perfectly good food any poor orphan would be thankful to get."

"Odd," I remarked.

"She's an odd one, all right."

I was disappointed. I had asked about Mrs. Hawke in hopes that the maid would indicate that Delia was really here, after all. Delia would have had an eyetooth pulled before intentionally stroking a cat. Derek Hawke had not been lying when he said the Mrs. Hawke Morris had referred to was an old woman.

"I meant the young Mrs. Hawke," I said hopefully. "Derek's wife."

"He ain't married," Betty retorted. "Though it ain't

surprisin'. No woman in her right mind would have
'im."

I got out of bed and pulled a white linen robe over
my nightgown. I smiled at Betty, hiding my disappointment. I intended to cultivate the woman. She
would be a marvelous source of information, for
clearly very little went on at Blackcrest that she didn't
know about. For all her sanctimonious pretension,
she had alert eyes and a lively tongue and she certainly had no scruples about discussing her employ-
ers. Betty plainly had a penchant for gossip, and later
on she might prove an important ally in my quest.

"I heard you talking with a young girl outside my
door," I said.

"Miss Honora? Yes, she was about to burst into
your room when I got upstairs. There's no controllin'
that child—although she ain't one of them wild ones,
mind you. An angel, she is, but with a mind of 'er
own, and that's puttin' it mildly."

"Is she Mr. Hawke's sister?" I inquired.

"Lord, no. She ain't nothin' like him, an' that's a
blessing. She's the old lady's legal ward. Poor thing,
her parents died when she was a baby, and the old
lady took 'er in, much like she'd of taken in a kitten
without a home. Miss Honora's parents were distant
relatives, and there was no one else. She's a love, she
is, a perfect love."

Betty's tone of voice left no doubt as to her feelings
toward the girl. She would have faced a firing squad
for Miss Honora, refusing the blindfold as a further
sign of loyalty. I found this quite touching.

"The master does get impatient," Betty said now as
I stood lingering in my robe and nightgown. "Per'aps

you'd better snap it up, ma'am. He does hate to wait. He begins to boil, if you know what I mean."

"I believe I do," I replied glibly.

"We all like to keep 'im in a good temper whenever possible. Makes things more pleasant an' all."

She made a wry face, indicating her personal opinion of the master. I smiled.

"I'll be downstairs dustin' the hall furniture," Betty said. "When you finish dressin', you'll find me there, an' I'll show you to the breakfast room."

"Thank you, Betty."

I took my time getting ready. Derek Hawke could simply boil. I intended to look my best. I brushed my hair until it had the deep coppery highlights. I applied makeup with extra care. Morris had brought up my suitcase, and I took out my emerald-green linen. It was old and no longer in fashion, but the cut was simple and the lines had an enduring chic that always looked up-to-date. The color went perfectly with my hair. I surveyed myself in the mirror before leaving the room. It might be hellishly early in the morning for style, but I felt I passed inspection. I could face Derek Hawke with composure.

I closed the door of my room and walked down the hall. I wasn't at all sure I could find my way to the staircase that led downstairs. I had been exhausted and bewildered last night when I followed the butler up, and we had turned several corners, leaving the main hall and going down a series of smaller ones. My room was in one of the wings, away from the main part of the house.

I turned a corner and stopped in bewilderment. I had come to a dead end. I started to retrace my way, when a door opened behind me. The girl came out.

She looked startled at seeing me, then relieved. She wore a dark blue sweater with a short pleated gray-and-blue tweed skirt. Honora did not seem to be in the least aware of her beauty, and that gave it an added quality of innocence and charm.

"Hello," she said. "I'm Honora."

"I'm Deborah. I seem to be lost."

"That isn't surprising," Honora replied. "Once we had a house guest who was lost for hours. We finally found her in one of the pantries. She thought it was a bathroom and the door slammed to and locked behind her. She was in an awful state when we found her. There were rats in the pantry—"

"How dreadful," I said.

"I was rather glad. She was a prissy old thing, a friend of Andy's who was being considered as a governess for me. She had warts."

"Warts?"

"One on her nose, two on her neck."

"Most unsuitable on a governess," I remarked.

"That's what I thought," Honora replied.

"Did you have many governesses?" I asked.

"A few. Then I was sent away to school. It was dreadful. There was no hot water, and all the other girls were great lumpy things full of adenoids, but I learned to drink tea properly and curtsy and read Molière in the original. I never thought I'd miss Blackcrest, but I did. I was ever so glad to get back. Jessie baked a special cake, and Betty said her baby had grown up—"

She smiled for a moment, remembering the episode, the smile lingering at the corners of her soft pink lips. Then her eyes grew cloudy. The smile vanished. She glanced quickly up and down the hall before stepping closer to me. She lowered her voice, as though afraid someone else might hear what she had to say.

"I'm glad we've met like this," she said, "before . . . before you go downstairs to talk to Derek. I don't know who you are, and I don't know why you're here, but I can tell you're—understanding."

"I'd like to think I am," I said.

"There is something I must ask you. I suppose you know what it is?"

"I can guess," I said quietly, "and you needn't worry. I won't say a word about seeing you last night."

Her enormous eyes regarded me nervously, as though she didn't dare believe me. I smiled reassuringly.

"He's a handsome lad," I said, "although the hair and black leather aren't exactly to my taste."

"That's all part of his—pose," she said. "He isn't like that at all, not like those others who hang around at the café. He's wonderful. He's working hard to make something of himself. Everyone else thinks he is insolent and sullen—"

"By 'everyone else,' you mean Derek Hawke?"

"How did you know?"

"I merely guessed," I replied.

"Derek thinks I'm a child. He sees me as some fragile doll he must keep wrapped up in tissue paper, away from the world. He almost had a fit when Andy bought me the Chevrolet. There wasn't anything he could do about it, though. He has no legal say-so over me, and Andy can put him down when she's a mind to. Andy's my guardian."

"Andy?"

"Andrea Hawke. She owns Blackcrest."

"I see."

"Derek hates Neil. He says Neil doesn't show proper respect. Neil lives here, you see, in the carriage house out in back. His father's our gardener. Neil helps him during the day, working on the grounds, and at night he works at the café-station. Neil's the only person I know who holds down two jobs. No one who works like that can be bad."

"It seems quite commendable," I agreed.

"I've known Neil all my life. He was like a brother to me when I was growing up. We fought all the time, and I thought he was a nasty little boy. Then, when I came back from school, all that—changed."

Her face was radiant as she spoke of the boy. It glowed with beauty that only one emotion can give. I remembered how intensely one feels everything at that age, how tragic and hopeless everything seems, and I sympathized with the girl in her love for the gardener's son.

"Derek thinks Neil is only interested in my money. Andy set up a trust fund for me, and there was quite a lot of insurance when my parents died. It'll all be mine when I turn eighteen. That's just a few months away. None of them will have any say over me then."

"Does your guardian object to your seeing the boy?" I asked.

"Andy? I don't think she's even aware of the way I feel about Neil. She's too wrapped up in her cats and committees and letters to the newspapers to pay much attention to me. Now she's writing her memoirs, and that takes up all her time. Oh, she's a dear, and I love her, but she's rather vague about everything. It's Derek who opposes it. He's forbidden me to speak to Neil. Neil's father is afraid Derek will fire him, so he's forbidden Neil to have anything to do with me. They're doing all they can to keep us apart."

"Surely you and your young man can wait?"

"That's what Neil says. But I can't—"

"A few months is a very short time."

"I won't wait," she said, her voice passionately intense. "There are things—"

She stopped abruptly. She composed herself. I could see the effort that took. I had the impression she had been on the verge of telling me something very important, of opening a closet door and revealing a skeleton so horrifying it would chill the blood. My pulses leaped. Could it have something to do with Delia? I felt it imperative to question the girl, but the moment had passed. She was cool and reserved now. Whatever secret she had been about to tell was locked away.

"You must forgive me," she said. "I . . . I've been very rude. No one likes to listen to the problems of other people. I don't ordinarily go on like this. It's just that . . . there are so few people to talk to, and you seem so nice, Deborah."

"That's the nicest compliment I've had in a long time," I replied.

"Will you be staying at Blackcrest long?" she asked.

"I don't know."

"It would be nice, but—"

"Yes?" I prompted.

"Nothing. Come, I'll show you the way down now."

We walked down the hall. The house was shabby here, the wallpaper peeling at the seams, the carpet worn and smelling of moths. Plaster flaked off the ceiling, and there were brown moisture stains. Honora led the way through the maze of halls, and we finally came to the main staircase that curved down to the front hall. The girl hesitated, her hand resting on the dark mahogany banister.

"I like you, Deborah," she said. "I . . . I do hope you'll keep your word and not mention seeing me last night."

"Of course I will," I replied.

It was dark at the top of the staircase. There were no windows anywhere near, and none of the sunlight penetrated here. Shadows stroked the dark blue wallpaper. Tall green plants grew in ugly black pots, their heavy leaves giving a dense, junglelike effect where we were. I could barely see the girl as she stood half-hidden by one of the plants.

"Are you one of Derek's friends?" she asked abruptly.

"I just met him last night," I replied.

"I'm glad. I'm . . . glad you're not his friend."

"Why do you say that?"

She hesitated. Once again she seemed about to reveal something important. She touched one of the blackish-green leaves, and when she finally spoke, her voice was so low I could hardly hear her.

"It isn't likely you'll stay," she said. "It's just as well. Derek doesn't like people here. I'm afraid Blackcrest isn't a happy place. You're much too nice to be here."

I wanted to ask her to explain her words, but she had gone. She had vanished among the shadows. I was alone, surrounded by the dark plants. What a very strange girl, I thought, and how very odd her last words. I hesitated for a moment and then started down the spiral staircase. I would think about Honora later on. Now I was interested to see what Derek Hawke had to say for himself this morning.

5

Derek Hawke was just putting down the telephone receiver when I stepped into the breakfast room. He set the instrument aside and smiled at me, nodding his head in greeting. He was wearing a pair of brown pants and a bulky knit sweater of dull gold. His hair was as untidy as it had been the night before, spilling over his forehead in thick black waves. There was a strength and vigor about him this morning that made me uncomfortable. He was like a healthy animal confined to a small space and deliberately restraining great energy.

He ignored me for a moment as he jotted something down on a pad. I felt weak as I smelled the heavenly odors of coffee and toast. I hadn't eaten in almost twenty-four hours.

"There," he said, putting down the pad and looking at me. "How are you this morning, Miss Lane?"

"Hungry," I said, despite myself.

"I'll have cook bring in some breakfast. We've got quite a lot to talk about, haven't we?"

"Undoubtedly."

Derek Hawke pressed a bell. After a moment a fat, belligerent-looking woman came shuffling into the room. Her steel-gray hair was done up in curlers, and her angry brown eyes glared at me. She wore a light blue uniform and a pair of tennis shoes. She clutched a yellow tabloid in one hand, and the other one held a half-eaten sweet roll. She was clearly put out at being interrupted in her reading.

"Another ax murder, Jessie?" Hawke inquired.

"Found a severed head in a vacant lot. Police suspect a schoolmaster."

"Well, if you don't mind waiting awhile to pore over the details, Miss Lane would like her breakfast now. I'll have another cup of coffee to keep her company. Hurry it up, too, Jessie. Miss Lane is hungry."

Jessie shot me a venomous look and shuffled out of the room. I felt highly uncomfortable.

"Will she put ground glass in my eggs?" I asked.

"Jessie's been with us for twenty years," Derek Hawke explained in a smooth voice. "She's a bit eccentric, a bit set in her ways, but we overlook that. No one can cook a roast or make a pudding to match hers. With help so hard to find nowadays, Jessie's a treasure. She knows it, too, which complicates matters. I'm afraid she's got us over a barrel."

"Frightening thought," I remarked.

He grinned. He seemed to be in a very agreeable mood this morning, gracious, expansive. I wondered what had caused the change.

"Did you sleep well?" he asked.

"Fairly. I thought I heard loud voices."

"You probably did. I had words with my aunt's ward. The girl's seventeen and thinks she can stay out at all hours without a fare-thee-well from anyone. I hope it didn't disturb you too much?"

"I was too exhausted to let it really bother me."

"You had quite a day yesterday, didn't you?"

"That's putting it mildly."

"And quite a shock, as well. I'm sorry about that. Here's Jessie. Put the tray down anywhere, Jessie. We'll help ourselves."

Jessie slammed the tray down on the sideboard with an unnecessary clatter and shuffled heavily out of the room. The door banged behind her with an ear-splitting retort.

"We generally eat at seven-thirty," he said, not at all perturbed by the cook's conduct. "Jessie reserves the time between eight and eleven for her tabloids and astrology charts. She doesn't like her routine disturbed."

"So I've noticed."

"Help yourself, Miss Lane."

I heaped my plate high with fluffy yellow scrambled eggs and curls of crisp bacon. Derek Hawke poured coffee into thick blue cups and set a rack of fresh toast on the table. He watched with an amused expression as I devoured my food, going back for a second helping of bacon. When I had finished he lit one of his slender brown cigars and strolled over to the window, pushing the curtain aside. I poured another cup of coffee. I felt strong now, ready for battle.

"It seems I owe you an apology," he began.

"Oh?"

"I'm convinced you're no blackmailer."

"How did you reach that cheerful conclusion, Mr. Hawke?"

"I've been on the telephone all morning," he said, "talking to some of my connections in London—a quite reliable firm, in fact."

"Indeed?"

"They did some checking up and called me back. The phone bill is going to be enormous, but it's been worth it. I've found out quite a lot about you, Miss Lane."

"Have you?"

He nodded. "It's amazing what you can learn if you put the right people on to it. I made my first call at seven, and within an hour and a half I learned all I needed to know about you."

"And what would that be?"

"First of all, that you're quite respectable and have no police record of any kind. Secondly, that you do indeed have a cousin named Delia Lane who left London a month ago with, supposedly, every intention of making a suitable marriage. It seems she didn't give the man's name to any of the people my man contacted, but they all agreed that she left to be married."

I waited, reserving any comment until he was finished.

"She quit the show she was with—*Mod Madness*, some kind of musical revue—and drew eleven hundred pounds out of the bank. The producer was furious and had some very unpleasant things to say about people who quit without proper notice. Miss Lane left London on April 14 and hasn't been heard from since."

"So?"

"I'm not finished. Miss Lane was seen once or twice

in the company of a tall, dark stranger—you'll pardon the expression—who might possibly resemble me in essentials. She didn't introduce this man to any of her friends. In fact, she went out of her way to keep his identity a secret. The choreographer of the revue met them in a pub and felt properly snubbed when she didn't introduce her companion."

"Is that all?"

"Not quite. It seems she told one of the chorus girls she was coming to Hawkestown and would live in a tremendous old house. That's all my man could uncover in such a short time, although he did pick up a few savory items about Miss Lane's romantic life."

"Really?"

"He's had no time to check any of this, mind you, but gossip has it that your cousin was hardly selective in her choice of male companions. She once dated a member of Parliament, married variety, but threw him over for a trombone player. Her name has been linked with a French film star, a bartender, a soccer player, and the proprietor of a left-wing bookstore in Chelsea. I'm sure there are others, but my man hasn't had time to discover them yet. His assistants are working on it."

"I'll just bet they are," I said angrily.

"Are the reports false?"

"You know how theater people gossip and backbite."

"Still, where there's smoke—"

"Are you suggesting that my cousin is promiscuous?"

"Not at all. I'm merely trying to corroborate my theory."

"And what would that be, Mr. Hawke?"

"It's quite simple. Your cousin met a man—married, no doubt—in London, probably a very rich and influential man, and decided to run off with him for a few weeks of holiday. It was important that no one knew his name, so she was extremely secretive about it. I've no doubt she'll turn up in a week or two with a glorious tan, a new mink coat, and a fund of anecdotes about the south of France."

"That's all very well," I said hastily, "but you don't know Delia. She's gone out with dozens of men—she's full of life and loves to play around—but she's quite moral. She's never accepted an expensive gift from any of her escorts, and she'd never run off with a married man. She hates the south of France. We both went there once for a week's holiday and met the most incredible bores. I blistered and Delia got diarrhea. I'm afraid it wouldn't hold water!"

Derek Hawke grinned. I blushed at the unintentional pun.

"Your theory," I snapped.

"I gathered as much."

"She told me about you," I said. "She described you and described Blackcrest. Explain that, and while you're at it, explain the telegram I showed you last night."

He took a glossy magazine from the sideboard and laid it on the table in front of me. It was an expensive periodical devoted to old homes and antiques. He opened it to an article about Blackcrest, complete with picture of the house and one of himself standing with an old woman holding a frilly parasol that shadowed both their faces.

"My aunt permitted this article, against my protests. She even dug up those old photographs and gave them to the editor. Your cousin could be vague and mysterious with her friends and co-workers, but she had to have some credible story to present to you. I suggest she saw this article and fabricated the whole thing, using this as a basis for her story to you."

"Mr. Hawke, if you knew my cousin, you would know how incredible it would be for her to so much as glance at a magazine like this. Her taste in reading matter resembles that of your cook."

"Nevertheless, she could have seen it."

"What about the telegram?"

"I've no doubt she sent it—perhaps even from Hawkestown—but the telegram was a decoy, sent to back up the story she'd handed you."

"I can't believe that," I replied.

Derek Hawke folded his arms across his chest and leaned against the wall, very much at ease. In the dull gold sweater he looked like a ski instructor. He watched me with his black-brown eyes, evidently waiting for further comment. I did not know what to say. I finished my coffee, setting the cup aside. I tried to formulate my thoughts.

The breakfast room was bright and cheerful and not at all like the rest of the house I had seen. The walls were papered with an off-white. Brown and yellow rag rugs were scattered over the brown parquet floor. A heavy linen tablecloth of dark gold covered the table, a thick white bowl of brown and yellow chrysanthemums placed in the middle. It was not easy to think about a foul crime as I sat in this pleasant room, but that was exactly what I was doing. The tall, casual stranger leaning against the wall looked as though he could murder an infant without blinking a lash.

"Your 'connections' in London seem to have found out quite a lot in a very short time," I said. "I find that remarkable."

"My man has several assistants. I told him expediency was vital. He put all his men on it. They can do wonders under pressure."

"So it would seem," I replied.

"You think I'm lying?"

"I think all this so-called information is, in fact, merely things you already knew, things Delia told you."

Derek Hawke frowned. He still leaned against the wall, but he was no longer casual and relaxed. He was tense, like an animal preparing to spring.

"You still maintain that I brought her here?"

"I . . . I don't know."

"What if I did?" he said calmly. "Supposing I lured her here with a promise of wealth and marriage. Supposing I managed to smuggle her into the house without anyone seeing us, throttled her, and then buried the body in the cellars—there is a great catacomb of cellars under Blackcrest, even a secret passage that leads out into the woods, the perfect place for a crime. If I had done this, Miss Lane, believe me I would have taken every precaution. There would be no way to prove it without digging up the cellars and uncovering the body—"

"That could be arranged," I retorted, interrupting him.

"Don't be absurd. Can you think of one single motive I would have for committing such a crime?"

"My cousin drew eleven hundred pounds out of the bank. That's not a small sum of money."

"Murder has been committed for less," he remarked. "Quite true. I can assure you I could put my hands on twice that sum merely by lifting this telephone. No, Miss Lane, the whole thing is absurd. I can sympathize with you in your concern, and I can understand your alarm. Your cousin has evidently lied to you and I've been the innocent tool of her lie. It's unpleasant, but those are the facts."

"I'm not so sure," I replied crisply.

"You intend to go to the police with your accusations?"

"I may."

"That would be foolish, Miss Lane," Derek Hawke said quietly.

He looked menacing. He moved away from the wall and came toward me with slow steps. He stopped a yard away from me and stood looking down at me. His eyes glowered. His wide lips were stretched tight. I felt a moment of sheer panic. This man was unscrupulous, and he was shrewd. He had worked everything out, down to the last little detail, and it would take superhuman control to fight him, to find out what he had done and then prove it.

"The police won't be able to help you," he said. "They will think the same thing I do—that your cousin has run away with some man after taking considerable pains to cover her tracks. They won't be able to prove a thing against me, and if you make your slanderous accusations against me, I'll see that my lawyers bring charges against you."

He stared at me for a moment longer and then shrugged his shoulders and stepped over to the sideboard. He was grinning as he poured another cup of coffee for each of us. He had won. He knew it.

"Try to see things clearly," he said.

"I believe I do."

"You think I'm a white-slaver, a murderer?"

"The facts—"

"The facts point to an irresponsible romantic escapade."

"Delia wouldn't lie to me. Not to me."

"It's absurd," he said. "Fantastic. Last night I was ready to believe you were a blackmailer, come to carry out some devious scheme. I was wrong about you. I will admit that. I have already apologized for what I thought. Surely you'll admit you were wrong about me."

I looked down at the tablecloth, thinking.

I fully realized the position I was in. Derek Hawke had everything in his favor. Delia had played right into his hands, even back in London. He had probably handed her some story about the need of keeping the romance a secret for a while, and she *had* been vague and mysterious. She had even neglected to bring him to meet me, which should have aroused my suspicions at once. Now everything fit together perfectly to suit Derek Hawke's theory, even the magazine article that Delia *could* have used to make up her story. Actresses were all supposedly irresponsible and immoral, and Delia *had* been slightly erratic in her love life. The police would believe what Hawke wanted them to believe. I was left with nothing but my own certainty that this man had done something dreadful.

He was not going to get away with it.

I could not go to the police yet, nor could I continue to make accusations against Derek Hawke if I intended to learn anything from him. I would have to take another approach. Perhaps all those expensive sessions at dramatic school would stand me in good stead now.

"Perhaps I was wrong," I said.

I deliberately made my voice weak and doubtful. I looked up at him with helpless eyes, eyes that appealed to him. It worked. I could see him melting toward me. He smiled in a satisfied male way and passed me the cup of fresh coffee.

"I just can't believe Delia would do such a thing," I said.

"We are frequently mistaken about those we're very close to," Derek Hawke replied. "I'm sure your cousin meant no real harm."

"Delia and I were so close—"

"It's always hard to realize the truth," he said.

"I'm so . . . worried."

"I can understand that," he said generously.

"I don't know what to do." I hoped I wasn't overplaying.

"Your cousin will turn up."

"Do you really think so?"

"Of course," he said kindly.

I thought he was going to pat my hand. I braced myself for the contact. I was mistaken. He swung a chair around to face the one I sat in and straddled it, his arms resting on the straight back. He smiled at me in the particular way men smile when they have bed in mind. Derek Hawke had an almost hypnotic magnetism, but I was on firm ground now. I could handle him, I thought. He was going to try to charm me out of my suspicions, charm me out of thinking all those ugly things about him. When he was done, I would be

ust another admiring female, ready to believe any-
hing he wanted me to believe.

It might have worked, had I not been playing the
;ame game.

6

It was going to be a most dangerous game. Derek Hawke would not be taken in by mere feminine wiles and flattery to his ego. I would have to play it very, very cool, with just the right balance of promise and reserve. If I seemed to promise too much too soon, he would be suspicious, guess my motives. If I was too reserved, he would lose interest altogether. I once played Mata Hari in an ill-fated comedy that closed after opening night in London. The present performance was going to have to be much more convincing than that one had been.

Derek Hawke shifted in his chair and looked at me with hooded lids. He seemed to be determining his chances. I fingered my coffee cup, my face full of worry and concern, attractively arranged. I raised my eyes to look at him. I tried to sound contrite.

"I do owe you an apology. I don't suppose it's every day a strange woman comes barging into your house and accuses you of—of something so unpleasant."

"Not every day," he admitted.

"I suppose I should contact the Bureau of Missing Persons," I said.

"I told my man in London to stay on the case," he said. "There are ways of checking such things—train tickets, hotel reservations, passport photographs, and so on. He'll do the job far better than any government bureau, far faster. Why don't we just let him handle it?"

He didn't want me to contact anyone about Delia. That was clear. He was afraid to have anyone investigate her disappearance, so he thought he would put me off with talk of this fictional "man" in London in hopes I would let things rest for a while.

"But I couldn't let you do that," I demurred. "It's not your concern. The expense—"

"The expense is negligible," he replied smoothly, "and I'm quite concerned. After all, it would seem I'm implicated in a dark crime. Let's just say I want my name cleared. No, I'll leave my man on the case. I have no doubt that before the week is out your cousin will be located in Majorca with a married millionaire."

"Majorca?"

"You said she hated the south of France."

"So I did."

"More coffee, Miss Lane?"

"No. I must be going. I . . . I suppose I can find a room in town? I may as well stay in Hawkestown for a few days. I've closed up the flat in London, and I have no job to go back to." This sounded properly sad and dejected. "I . . . I want to be nearby so you can contact me the minute your man has any news."

He started to make some reply, but at that moment

the door flew open and a woman came rushing into the room. At first I thought it was Jessie come to claim her revenge, and I gave a little start. The woman who hurried across the room was only slightly less alarming than the vindictive cook would have been. She was short and rotund, with a chubby face dominated by the liveliest blue eyes I had ever seen. Her cheeks were vividly flushed, her small lips were pursed with alarm, and her whole demeanor was that of one come to announce the house afire. Her apparel was not to be believed.

"Yes, Andy?" Derek Hawke asked calmly.

"The ginger kitten! It's run off again. I think it's in the cellars. Someone's left the cellar door open again —I know it was Jessie! She's been sneaking up bottles of wine again. You've got to do something about that, Derek. After all, that wine is pure vintage. Stephen brought it from France before the Great War—" She paused, her wide eyes suddenly blank, as though she'd lost track of what she was saying.

"The kitten? Yes! I went to their room, and it's frightfully cold, Derek. That's why I'm wearing this coat—" A huge, slightly tattered fur coat covered her short body. Beneath it I caught glimpses of a smock, psychedelic in effect, hot pink and orange, purple and red. A scarf of violent blue silk was tied loosely around short, fluffy black curls that were surely silver by nature. "What were you saying?" she demanded in an angry tone, staring at her nephew with petulant impatience. "You know my time is valuable, Derek, and really, these interviews—"

"Not a thing, Andy," Derek Hawke said mildly.

"Then why—oh, yes. The kittens' room—I call them all kittens," this to me, "although most of them are quite grown. It's freezing. The heating has gone out, and you know how cold it gets down there. The poor things will have to *chop* their water. You must do something about that, Derek. Someone has to show some responsibility around here. Yes, and the cellars? Did you say something about the cellars?"

"The ginger kitten," her nephew suggested.

"He's such a frisky little thing. I think it's psychological. He's the only ginger in the bunch, and all the rest are black and brown and white. One marmalade, although she's far too hateful and mean to have any feelings of inferiority. The dear has run off, Derek. I saw him running down the hall, and then he just *vanished*. That's when I discovered the cellar door. I don't know what Jessie can be thinking of. She does it on the sly, of course, and we have no proof yet, but—"

Derek Hawke sighed tolerantly. His aunt wrapped the tattered fur about her and tapped her foot. Neither of them spoke for a moment.

"Well, are you going to send Morris to search, or do you intend to let the kitten die? I know, Derek, that you don't particularly *care* for them, but that's no excuse for criminal neglect. He wouldn't last a day down there—"

"Relax, Andy. We haven't lost a kitten yet."

"No thanks to *you*, I'm sure," she said frostily.

Derek Hawke rose with a gesture of resignation and summoned Morris. The butler listened with a martyred expression while Hawke gave him instructions to search for the missing kitten. As he left the room, Morris glanced at the old woman and shook his head. Andrea Hawke drew herself up regally, tossing the skirt of the coat as though it were a part of the coronation robes.

"Morris is getting a bit uppity," she remarked casually. "Don't you feel, Derek? I may be forgetful at times, but I don't intend to tolerate insolence from anyone. Now, that's done. Morris will find the kitten. He may as well earn his wages some way—and Neil can see about the heating. He's so clever with things like that. Speak to him, Derek. I want the heat turned on down there immediately."

"I won't have that boy inside the house," Derek Hawke replied.

"Nonsense. He's a perfect dear—so attractive, though he could use a haircut. You must get over this class thing, dear. Just because he's the gardener's son doesn't mean he can't fix our heating. One can't draw so fine a line with servants nowadays, though of course there *was* a day when I wouldn't have dreamed of asking outside help to come inside. One must change with the changing times, and I certainly won't have *you* messing around with the heating unit. All that gas, and your cigars—I can visualize the horror. Tell Neil to attend to it at once, dear. Now, I will take the young lady and show her her room. Selfish of you not to have told me she'd arrived. I've been waiting for three days—"

"Andy, this isn't—"

"What's your name, dear?" Andrea Hawke asked, ignoring her nephew.

"Deborah Lane."

"Lane? A lovely name. I knew some Lanes once. Such a dear family they were. The father died of calcium deposits—have you ever heard of such a thing? Do you type?"

"Type?"

"I suppose you modern girls prefer those electrical

machines, don't you? Well, I don't have one. They terrify me. You won't need to know shorthand, of course, but I do hope you can read my handwriting. Honora says it looks like someone's dipped a chicken's foot in ink and turned it loose on paper. Cruel thing for a child to say, but I'm afraid there is a bit of truth in it. I do hope you'll work out. At least you don't have bumps. The employment agency sent me a girl a few years ago who had the most ghastly bumps. She *picked* them at her desk. Of course, I had to let her go. Most unsanitary for the kittens."

"Andy," Derek Hawke said firmly, "Miss Lane is not from the employment agency. You seem to be confused—"

"Don't be absurd, Derek. You're the one who's confusing things with all this talk about calcium deposits."

"Miss Lane is not from the employment agency," he repeated.

"I distinctly told you a week ago I needed a girl to help me type up the completed chapters of my memoirs. The publishers simply refuse to look at anything not typed. I know I told you to contact the employment people because I jotted it down on my pad right under the message about beets. 'Tell Jessie no beets on menu,' 'no' underlined. 'Tell Derek to send for temp. sec.' I can see it now. I must have told you, because she's here, isn't she?"

"Not for that purpose," he said, his voice determined.

"She's just told us she's a marvelous typist, dear. If it's a question of salary, I won't split hairs. After all, it *is* my money, even if you do yell every time I send a donation to H.F.U.M."

"H.F.U.M.?" I said, unable to restrain myself.

"Home for unwed mothers. It's a class thing, again, but one must do something to help. Now, Miss Lane, what did you have in mind for wages? I'll be reasonable about it, of course, but I don't intend to be robbed. Shall we say—"

"Andy," Derek Hawke said loudly, "Miss Lane is not a secretary."

Andrea Hawke stared at her nephew with reproach. "You don't have to shout, dear, I'm sure. None of us are wearing hearing aids. What will the servants think if we don't set a good example? Miss Lane," she said firmly, turning to me, "*do* you type?"

"As a matter of fact, I do," I replied.

"There," Andrea Hawke said, throwing her nephew a look of triumph. "The fact that you're my nephew and heir does entitle you to certain liberties, Derek, but they hardly extend to calling me a liar in my own house. I won't ask for an apology now. I haven't the time. Miss Lane can begin her duties immediately."

Derek Hawke walked over to his aunt and placed his hands firmly on her shoulders. He bent down so that his face was level with hers. When he spoke, his voice was level and controlled, but it was filled with irritation nevertheless.

"Miss Lane is an actress, Miss Lane came from London to see me on a personal matter. Miss Lane is not, repeat, *not* a secretary, and she was not sent from the employment agency."

Andrea Hawke looked stunned, then distressed.

"Why didn't you say so in the first place, Derek? No wonder I can't keep track of things around here. Did you send for a girl?"

"You never asked me to send for one."

"Miss Lane," she said, "I must apologize. You must think I'm mad. Most people do, as a matter of fact. Not certifiably, of course, or Derek would have already carted me away to the bin and seized the money. As it is, he'll have to wait. Well—" She sighed, holding her hands out in a gesture of resignation. "Now what shall we do? I suppose I'll have to wait weeks for Derek to remember to send for a girl, and then she'll probably have bumps again. You *do* type, Miss Lane?"

"Miss Lane is not interested in a job," Hawke said quickly.

"Let her speak for herself, Derek."

Her voice was a charming lilt, but it carried unmistakable authority. She made an outrageous figure as she stood there with the tattered fur coat half-covering the violently colored smock. I had been stunned at first, but now the eccentric clothes did not seem to matter. She was fluttery and forgetful, and her conduct probably caused deep grievances in the household, but she was in command, and she knew it. Andrea Hawke had the money, therefore the power, and no one would push her around, not even her nephew.

"I once worked as a secretary to a taxidermist," I said, truthfully enough. I held the job for three weeks at the age of nineteen until the atmosphere of the place drove me away.

"A taxidermist! I'm against them. Definitely. Dreadful, dreadful state when poor beasts—" She paused, looked at me with a twinkle in her blue eyes, then smiled. "It must have been stuffy work," she said, her voice dry.

"Quite," I said, appreciative. Andrea Hawke wasn't as slow on the uptake as I had first assumed.

"You don't *believe* in it, do you?" she asked.

"Definitely not. Dreadful business."

"Would you like to work for a slightly befuddled old lady? I have quite a few cats, but they're all alive and kicking—"

"Aunt Andrea," Hawke protested, his voice menacing, "I must insist—"

Andrea Hawke turned to me with a charming smile. "Derek is against the whole idea of my writing these memoirs," she said, as though speaking of a naughty child. "He's afraid I'll tell all the family secrets. He's so right! Scandal sells—look at those disgusting books my other nephew writes—and there are some delicious scandals to reveal. Did I ever tell you about the countess who stayed here in 1804 and left with a suitcase full of silver—*and* the coachman my great-great-grandmother on Daddy's side had just trained? All the first part of the book is devoted to those randy days before I was born. Randy? Is that a proper word to use?"

"It'll do nicely," I said.

"Miss Lane," Derek Hawke said. He looked at me with a grim expression.

He had frowned when I mentioned my abilities at the typewriter, and he had grown increasingly more grim after my reference to the job with the taxidermist. He guessed my plan, and he didn't like it. He didn't trust me. That was just too bad. I couldn't afford to let an opportunity like this go by. I had intended to stay in Hawkestown and find out as much as I could there. The opportunity to stay at Blackcrest itself was not to be missed, even if Derek Hawke was

uspicious of my motives. I looked at him with wide
:yes and gave him my most beseeching smile.

"To be perfectly frank, I could use the job," I said.
And I would be on hand in case there were any developments—"

"Developments?" Andrea Hawke said.

Her nephew went pale. He gave me a frantic signal.
knew I had won the first round. He did not want his
aunt to know what had happened and would do anything to keep the information from her, even if it
meant he must let me take the job. The room was
silent. Derek Hawke was fuming, very much in con-
rol of himself and determined to hide it from his
aunt, yet fuming. He tapped his fingers on the yellow
'lecloth. His eyes were burning as they held mine.

"Developments?" Andrea Hawke repeated, impa-
:ient now. She didn't miss much, despite her absent-
minded chatter and apparently fuzzy comprehension.
Behind that frivolous facade Andrea Hawke was as
hard as nails, I thought. Her nephew was wary of her,
and I felt sure he had good reason to be.

"I think Miss Lane might be ideally suited for the
job," he said. This was spoken very slowly, and his
eyes never left mine.

"That's what I've been trying to tell you, dear," she
exclaimed, thoroughly delighted now. "She'll be able
to help me with my vocabulary, too, Derek. What a
divine idea this was!" She took my hand in hers and
pulled me toward the door. "Now, don't forget to
speak to Neil about the heating unit, and you must
remind me to have a long talk with Jessie about the
wine. Come, Miss Lane. You're going to be delighted
with the room I've chosen for you. I *do* hope you like
cats."

"I adore them," I lied.

Derek Hawke seemed about to say something more. He restrained himself. He was standing silently by the table when we left the room.

7

Andrea Hawke was laughing to herself as we left the room. I was reminded of a mischievous child who has just won a squabble. I figured that Andrea Hawke won most of the arguments she participated in. Her method of defeating her foe might be startling, but I had no doubt she was always ultimately the victor. In her own fuzzy way she was a dynamic creature. I would never make the mistake of underestimating her.

She hurried down the hall, the fur coat flapping dustily, flashes of bright psychedelic color swirling about her knees. We turned a corner and began moving down a long corridor. One side was solid wall covered with dark oak paneling, and the other was made up of a row of windows that looked out over the gardens. The windowpanes were dirty, and there were no curtains. A few of the panes were broken. I was surprised to see cobwebs stretched silkily across the top corners of several. The odor of dust, decay, and mildew was overwhelming.

"Blackcrest is so large," Andrea Hawke said chattily as we sailed along the corridor, "it's impossible to keep order—the girls are terribly fussy. Betty and Agnes, you know, just two, one for up, one for down, and then there's Morris. They complain constantly, but they manage to keep the bedrooms and the main rooms downstairs in shape. All the rest of the house is shambles, just shambles, sheets over the furniture and dust an inch thick on the chandeliers. But we've held on—taxes are abominable. Thieves in the government. Why should *I* pay for planes and missiles? Don't you agree?"

"Indubitably."

"We've held on. Remarkable, in this day and age. I would *die* before I'd open the place to tourists. So many of our best families—for half a crown they think they can litter the place with orange peels and paper cups and stick wads of chewing gum on William Morris paper. Not in my house, thank you!"

"It's a fascinating place," I told her rather breathlessly. We were practically running down the corridor.

"Naturally. The tales these walls could tell! You'll learn a lot when you type up the memoirs, of course. I do adore your hair, child. It's the color of sunset over the desert. Now we turn here. Watch your step. Do you like towers?"

"I've never been in one."

"That's ridiculous. Not even in London? All that talk about the little princes. Rot! He didn't do it. Not with those eyes—"

"I adored Olivier," I said.

Andrea Hawke stopped abruptly, so abruptly that I almost ran into her. She whirled around to face me. There was a curious twinkle in her blue eyes. A strange little smile played on her bright pink lips.

"You are sharp, aren't you?" she said. "Not many people are able to follow me. They say I'm scatter-brained—"

"Not at all," I replied soberly. "Towers, the little princes, Sir Laurence as Richard the Third. It's a matter of mental reflex, wouldn't you say? I suppose most people are rather slow—"

"Remarkable," she said, "absolutely remarkable. You and I are going to get along famously. Why didn't Derek want you to work for me? I would think he'd be delighted to have a gorgeous creature like you about the place."

"I don't think he trusts me," I replied.

"Oh, well, he doesn't trust anyone. Ever since—but that's in the past, yet one would think—"

I waited, curious to learn what had happened to cause Derek Hawke to be so wary of everyone. Andrea merely shook her head, privately reflecting on the incident and clearly not intending to discuss it with me at the moment. I curbed an impulse to question her about it. It would not be wise to be too pressing just yet. I was going to stay at Blackcrest, and there would be plenty of time to uncover all the family secrets. I expected Betty to be a great help.

"Towers? Yes, I was going to tell you about the tower. It's mine. I mean, of course all of Blackcrest is mine, naturally, and will be until Derek takes over, but the tower is particularly mine. The cats, you understand. Betty and Agnes won't abide them, and Jessie would toss a grand fit if one of them pranced into the kitchen. I have to keep them away, and the tower is ideal. It's a ruin, but cozy. I think you'll like your room."

"In the tower?" I asked.

"Yes, over the cats and the study. I have the master bedroom. It's Regency and rather dull, but I have to stay there. I couldn't *sleep* in the tower. People would think me peculiar."

I remained discreetly silent on this point.

"But I spend most of my time there," she continued. "Come, I'll show you."

We walked down a dark, narrow little hall and came to a flight of flimsy wooden stairs that led down to what I assumed was the basement. I felt drafts of cold air swirling up to meet us as we descended. I understood the fur coat now. We reached the concrete floor. I could barely see the damp walls with pipes running along them. We seemed to be in a vast subterranean dungeon.

Andrea Hawke fumbled along one wall and touched a switch. A naked light bulb hanging overhead came to life, illuminating the area. I saw something large and gray scurrying along the floor and gave a little cry as it disappeared.

"Rats," Andrea said, shaking her head in exasperation. "The cats help a little, but I'm afraid there're just too many of them. You aren't going to be alarmed, are you?"

"N-no," I stammered.

"They're harmless, really. Come. This is the basement. That hall leads to the cellar door. The cellars go on forever, so damp and cold. The kitten will be petrified if Morris doesn't find it. We keep all the rubbish and rejects in the basement, and the cellars are lower, entirely underground. No one goes down there, besides Jessie, of course. We have a magnificent stock of wine, you see, and she nips. The tower is this way. . . ."

We walked down a long, damp hall away from the direction Andrea had pointed. I felt the sagging weight of Blackcrest overhead and wondered if the ceiling would collapse. Bits of plaster hung down, and the beams looked rotten. At the end of the hall there was a large area with part of a circular wall visible. A heavy oak door was in the middle of the wall, and to one side I could see a walled-in staircase winding up into the darkness. This must be the bottom room of the tower, I thought.

"There were once six rooms," Andrea explained. "But time and ruin, you know. The top three rooms simply aren't there anymore, just the outside wall, and bricks dropping from it every day. The cats stay down here in the basement room. Can you hear them?"

I nodded. From behind the oak door I could hear a screeching din. Andrea cocked her head to one side and smiled. Stacks of chipped purple dishes stood beside the door, and I noticed two unopened cartons of cat food, the most expensive kind. That explained the rats. What cat in his right mind would hunt rats when he could get food like that without effort, I reflected. The creatures inside seemed to be aware of Andrea's presence. They began scratching at the door, and the mewing took on an unmistakably plaintive note.

"We won't disturb them now," Andrea said. "You must be anxious to see the study and your room."

She hesitated. We heard footsteps coming down the hall toward us. There was something decidedly sinis-

ter about the sound, I thought. The basement was full
of echoes. Even as we spoke in normal voices I could
hear the walls tossing back the sound with soft embel-
lishments that made me uncomfortable. I peered into
the darkness at the other end of the hall. I could
barely see a dark figure moving toward the pool of
light spilled from the single naked bulb.

It was the boy called Neil. He wore a pair of tight
denim pants and a black sweat shirt. The heavy blond
hair was like a lion's mane. When he saw me, he
paused, obviously startled. For a moment he looked
very young and vulnerable, about to retreat back into
the shadows, and then his dark eyes grew flat and
expressionless and he continued toward us with an
exaggerated swagger. He carried a toolbox at his side.
Andrea fluttered, delighted to see him.

"Here you are! The cats are freezing, Neil. This is
Miss Lane, my new secretary. Neil's planning to go to
Oxford. *Must* you wear your hair like that, child? I
suppose it's a symbol. Everything's a symbol nowadays. Masculinity? Samson, you know—"

"Hello again," I said quietly.

"How do you do," he said. His voice was very polite
and formal. He stared at me for a moment with expressionless eyes, then turned all his attention on Andrea.

"I've come about the heating unit," he said.

"Of course. It's gone out again. The gas pilot, I suppose. Something's wrong with it. The poor angels
have been shivering all morning. Neil's so handy with
these things," she told me. "I can't imagine why he
wants to waste his time at Oxford. What we need is
people who can *do* things. Everyone can read Latin

nowadays, but no one can repair a stone wall or fix a leaky faucet—"

"I have the tools," he said, interrupting her.

"Oh? Tools?"

"The heating unit," he replied.

"Hurry along," she said peevishly. "The cats are freezing, and you stand here making idle conversation."

Neil stepped into the tower room, opening the door cautiously. I saw a swarm of furry creatures before he closed the door. Andrea led me to the stone staircase that wound up around the tower rooms. The steps were steep, and there was hardly enough room for one person to move between the outside wall and the wall of the room. It was damp and dark, and there was no railing. I could smell moss and lichen. When I touched the wall, it felt slimy. We reached a small landing, and Andrea opened the door to a room identical in size and shape to the one below.

"This is the study," she said, leading me inside. "Here's where I write and compose my letters and get away from everyone. It's messy—I have forbidden Agnes and Betty to touch anything—but it's all mine."

The room was perfectly round, surprisingly large, yet snug and intimate. The walls were plaster, painted a dull brown, with three narrow windows set high up, mere slits that would afford little light. An old sofa covered with worn orange velvet sat to one side, the springs sagging in the middle, its surface littered with newspapers and books, a brown cup and saucer perched precariously on one arm. A rolltop desk, incredibly cluttered, sat beneath one of the window slits, a tall lamp with a beaded shade standing beside it. There was a blue chair, a footstool to match, a plump tailor's dummy, a tarnished golden harp, and a table laden with priceless Dresden figurines. One could hardly take a step without stumbling over piles of books and magazines.

For all its disarray, the room had personality. I stepped over to the wall to examine a print that I was sure was an original Hogarth. A delicious smell of lavender pervaded the whole room, mixed with something I thought must be peat moss.

"Here they are," Andrea said, picking up a stack of lined yellow tablets that sat on the desk beside an ancient typewriter. In the various compartments of the desk top were letters, news clippings, oil cans, glue, fountain pens, pill bottles, and a gorgeously bejeweled snuffbox. It might have been a Fabérgé. Andrea waved the tablets.

"My memoirs," she said proudly. "They're going to shock the pants off the natives! So delightful! Such a lot of typing to do. You shall have your own hours. All I want is to see that the typing is done. Can you manage it in a week?"

"I'm certain of it," I replied.

"A few hours during the day. I'm sure there are many other things you'll want to be doing, and I don't believe in sweatshop labor."

"As a matter of fact, I *am* interested in exploring Hawkestown."

"What ever for? It's a dreadful place, not an interesting person in the lot, and such abominable shops. The Tea Shoppe used to be rather nice until that awful woman was hired as hostess. Tottie? You can't convince me that anyone is actually named Tottie."

I murmured some reply. The name on the cover of

one of the books at my feet caused me to lose track of what Andrea was saying.

"My nephew actually *sees* her. Can you imagine anything so scandalous?"

"Derek?"

"No, no. He wouldn't pass the time of day with such a loathsome person. Alex."

"Alex," I said.

I picked the book up. It was called *Bloodstains on Bella,* and the author was Alexander Tanner. On the back of the jacket there was a photograph of the man who had changed my flat tire the night before. He was wearing a tweed jacket, a pipe in his hand, his hair windblown. There was a wry grin on his wide mouth, as though he considered the whole bit a marvelous lark.

I knew now why his name had sounded familiar. He was the author of innumerable popular thrillers, and Delia had devoured them by the dozen. Copies of his books had littered the flat, and though I had never read one of them, I had listened to Delia babble excitedly about them all. He was her favorite author, the only one she read regularly.

"He wrote that dreadful thing," Andrea informed me. "Such garbage! A homicidal maniac who butchers men every time there's a full moon! Perfectly disgraceful!"

"Alex Tanner is your nephew?"

"Haven't you been listening to me, dear? I just told you—"

What a coincidence, I said to myself.

"Every time one of them is published, he sends half a dozen copies to Blackcrest. I know he does it just to aggravate me! As if I could ever bring myself to read such—well, occasionally, just to see what horrors he can imagine. Alex and I do *not* get along, not at all. And now that he's taken up with this Tottie—"

"Tottie?"

"The tea hostess."

"Oh."

"Derek can't stand him! Every time Alex comes to Blackcrest, there's a quarrel. Jessie adores him, of course. He dedicated one of his books to her. Every time he comes, she cooks the most divine meals. He actually tried to lure her to his cottage—"

"Jessie?" I said, horrified.

"To cook for him. Tried to steal her right out from under my nose. Shocking conduct."

"I should say so."

"He's just like his mother—irresponsible, flip, irreverent. He drives around in that shocking red car and thumbs his nose at everyone. And writing those books—"

I studied the photograph. There was a strong family resemblance between Alex Tanner and his cousin Derek. Each had the wide mouth, the twisted nose, the dark eyes and unruly hair, but whereas Derek Hawke was hard, angular, stern, Alex Tanner appeared loose and relaxed, wry and good-natured. Derek Hawke's hair was jet black, and I remembered his cousin's as being a rich brown. Hawke's eyes were piercing, while Alex's were friendly and warm; yet the fact that they both came from the same family pattern was quite evident.

I commented on this, and with typical verbosity and conversational excursions, Andrea Hawke explained the relationship. Her husband, Stephen Hawke, had a younger brother, Vincent, who was

Derek's father, and a sister, Marcia, who married a ne'er-do-well named Tanner and gave birth to Alex. The Tanners were family outcasts, spending most of their time in Nice and Cannes and squandering money outrageously. Their son had every one of their bad qualities, plus some of his own. His parents were dead now, but he managed to carry on in the grand tradition, *i.e.*, scandalously. Derek came to Blackcrest when his parents died, and he was going to inherit everything.

"But isn't that unfair to Alex?" I inquired.

"Unfair? That that scoundrel should get a penny from me! He laughs at Blackcrest. That young wastrel shall reap exactly what he's sown!"

"Which should be quite a sum," I remarked. "I would imagine the royalties on his books are staggering."

"Shocking," she said, shaking her head, "quite shocking. But we mustn't waste time talking about him. I'll show you your room now."

We went up the dark, twisting staircase again. I almost slipped on one of the stairs, but Andrea ran blithely up them, chattering about the room we were to see. I was rather dubious about it after seeing the one we had just left, but I was pleasantly surprised. The walls were painted a light blue, and there was a worn dark blue carpet on the floor. The bed had an enormous headboard of carved black wood and a counterpane of burnt orange satin. There was an overstuffed chair, a dressing table and mirror, a large carved black wardrobe. A vase of vivid orange marigolds sat on the dresser.

"It's delightful," I said. "There's an extra door—"

Andrea opened it and pointed down a long hallway

which she told me was the west wing of the house. This bedroom was the only tower room to connect with the rest of Blackcrest, and I could come and go in the house without going up and down the spooky staircase every time I wanted to go somewhere.

"You won't be afraid, will you?" she asked.

"Afraid? Why should I be?"

"It's so isolated—away from everyone else. The tower, the staircase, the basement and cellars—all so" —she searched for the proper word—"so . . . scary."

"Not at all. I'll adore the privacy."

"There are noises, of course. The wind, you know. It blows through the cracks in the outside wall and makes it sound as though someone were creeping up the stairs. I *could* give you another room."

"I wouldn't think of it."

"Betty has agreed to do your room every morning. You'll dine with us, of course."

"Uh—not tonight," I replied hastily. "I have an appointment. An old friend is meeting me in Hawkestown." I did not intend to tell Andrea Hawke that I had a dinner engagement with her disgraceful nephew.

"That's fine, dear. Now . . ."

We discussed the work, and I agreed to start on the memoirs after lunch. At my request, Betty brought a tray to my room. Morris brought my suitcase to the tower. I gave him my car keys so that the car could be moved to the garage in back of the house. After lunch I changed into sweater and slacks and joined Andrea in the study. I had some difficulty in reading her handwriting, but after a while I was able to decipher it. By five o'clock I had typed the whole first chapter, and Andrea was delighted as she read her words neatly typed on bond paper, clipped into a black cardboard cover. She left the room, and I spent the next fifteen minutes tidying the desk and setting things up for tomorrow's work session.

I was standing in front of the study door ready to go up to my room when Derek Hawke stepped onto the landing. He was still wearing the dull gold sweater. He didn't say anything for a moment. He stood with his arms folded across his chest, regarding me with narrowed eyes. I was exhausted after four hours of typing, and in no mood for verbal gymnastics. I started to move past him. He sidestepped quickly and blocked my way. That was getting to be a habit with him. I frowned.

"Finished already?" he asked.

"We've completed the first chapter."

"Remarkable. You really *can* type."

"Did you think I was lying?"

"I don't know," he replied slowly, his eyes on mine.

"If you don't mind, Mr. Hawke," I said irritably, "I am tired and rather anxious to get up to my room."

"By all means," he said, stepping aside and making a mock bow like an eighteenth-century gallant. "Andy is quite pleased with your work, Miss Lane. I do hope you don't regret your decision to remain at Blackcrest."

I had already started up the staircase. I turned and stared down at him.

"Regret it? Why should I?"

Derek Hawke smiled. It was not at all pleasant. "That remains to be seen," he replied.

He chuckled softly. The sound of it echoed against the walls and followed me as I hurried up the dark spiral staircase.

8

The waiter led me through an almost empty room. I noticed the enormous fireplace, a copper tub filled with logs sitting on the hearth. Beams of smoky blackwood supported the low ceiling, and ancient shields hung on the dark paneled walls. Candles with green glass shades burned at a few of the tables, casting long shadows. Music played softly, making a background for low voices and an occasional tinkle of glass.

I was nervous and ill at ease. I was not in the habit of accepting dinner invitations from men I'd just met, and learning what I had about Alex Tanner made me all the more wary. I had to confide in someone, and he was a member of the family. I had dressed carefully in a dark orange frock with short, flaring skirt. I followed the waiter, wondering if I shouldn't drop the whole thing and return to Blackcrest.

There was a rough wooden terrace in back. Rustic tables and chairs were placed beneath Japanese lanterns strung from the branches of the oak trees. The river ran directly behind the terrace. I could hear it washing along the banks. Only a few people sat beneath the bobbing colored shadows cast by the lanterns. Alex Tanner was sitting near the railing, looking out over the river. He did not see me approach.

"I'm ten minutes early," I said. "It's one of my idiosyncrasies—arriving early."

He leaped to his feet. A smile of pleasure spread on his face. He was wearing a gray-and-white-checked sport coat and a dark green tie. A lock of rich brown hair had fallen on his forehead, giving him a boyish appeal. He took my hand. His charm was almost tangible.

"Only when I'm looking forward to something, though," I added.

"You were looking forward to this?" He helped me to my seat.

"Surprisingly—yes."

He sat down, still smiling. "Why surprisingly?" he asked.

"I don't usually accept pickups."

"Must you think of it as that?" he asked. "I feel like I've known you for ever so long—I suppose it's seeing you on the screen. I've not thought of anything but this meeting since last night."

"You were sure I'd come?" I inquired.

"Naturally," he replied, grinning.

"Conceited of you," I said lightly.

"Women have made me that way," he retorted.

"I'll bet they have," I remarked.

The waiter came to take our order. I refused a cocktail, insisting that Alex go ahead and have one. He shook his head politely and ordered our meal. We chatted lightly after the waiter left. I commented on the restaurant, and he made a few remarks about the quality of the food. By the time the food arrived, I felt completely relaxed. There was something about Alex Tanner that put one immediately at ease. I wondered how many women had felt this way. Plenty, I thought.

"I understand you're a man of mystery," I said when we had finished the first course.

"Oh? How so?"

"Bloodstains on Bella," I replied.

"You found out about that. I hope you didn't read it?"

"I didn't," I admitted.

"Good. I'd hate for you to get the wrong impression of me. I write those things in about five weeks—I have no talent, but I've got the bloodiest imagination in captivity. They're not art, but they keep me in caviar."

"Are they all mysteries?" I inquired.

He nodded. "Murder and mayhem, dastardly villains and pretty young girls who keep on being chaste all over the English countryside."

"I think I've got a new plot for you," I said.

"Really?"

"Girl vanishes. She tells all her friends she is going to get married, then leaves town and is never heard from again."

He laughed quietly, his brown eyes glowing. "I've used it already in an epic called *Strangler of the Moors.* The girl was actually leaving for an illicit rendezvous with a handsome stranger she'd met in a pub. He was actually an escapee from a lunatic asylum who had a yen for young ladies with blond hair and trusting dispositions. It was one of my biggest sellers."

"What happened to the girl?" I asked.

"You really want to know?"

"I'm very interested."

He went on to give me some of the more gruesome details, telling me about the various murders. His voice was beautifully modulated, and he spoke lightly, making fun of the plot and people he had created. I could feel the color leaving my face as he described the climactic chase over the moors. I did not visualize Alex's blond, blue-eyed heroine pursued by the villain. I saw a girl with short red curls, an outrageous dimple on her left cheek, terror in her brown eyes. He might as well have been talking about Delia.

He looked up at me. He cut himself short.

"Is anything wrong?"

"No. Nothing at all."

"Come on—" he said, frowning. "Suddenly your face grows pale, and your voice quivers. What is it?"

"Your description is . . . very vivid."

"I didn't take you for a girl with such delicate sensibilities. All the talk about blood and gore upsets you?"

"It isn't that," I replied, rather irritated that he should think I was so fragile I would turn pale at the mention of blood.

"What is it, then? Look, I don't have dandruff on my shoulders, do I? I saw a commercial on television where a girl turns pale—" He was trying to make light of it. I smiled at the effort.

"I'm fine now," I said, "and you don't have dandruff."

"That's a relief. You sure there isn't something you want to tell me?"

"Not at the moment."

"Later?"

"Perhaps."

"You are the mysterious one."

"Do you mind?"

"I'm intrigued," he said.

We finished our meal, talking casually about unimportant things. I found that I was enjoying myself, despite my problem, and I warmed toward this man who was so witty, so wry, and yet so sincere. I felt that we might really have been friends for a long time. I wondered whether I should confide in him or not. I had a desperate need to tell someone about Delia, and yet this man was Derek Hawke's cousin.

I delayed the decision for a while. He questioned me about the film industry and didn't seem to be at all disappointed that I wasn't a real celebrity. He told me about some of his experiences with his publishers and talked quite humorously about a series of lectures he had given in London to groups of ladies in flowered hats who had an insatiable fascination with murders, the bloodier the better.

"They hung on my every word," he said.

"People are curious," I remarked.

"I know I am," he admitted. "About you. I wonder what a glamorous creature like you is doing in Hawkestown. Last night you told me you were coming to visit a relative, and yet you haven't mentioned a sister or a brother, an aunt or uncle. I have the suspicion that you're here on a secret mission, that there is no relative at all."

"You're right about the last part," I said. "There is no relative."

"Oh?"

"That's my problem."

"How so?" he inquired, propping his elbows casually on the table. There was a look of expectation in his warm brown eyes, a slight smile on his wide lips. He clearly expected to hear some frivolous, feminine story. I took a deep breath.

"I'm not sure I should tell you about it," I said.

"Why not?"

"I have my reasons."

"Try me," he said. "I'm an excellent listener."

I hesitated only a moment. "Very well . . ."

I told him everything, starting with the night Delia had first come in and told me about the marvelous man she'd met at a party in Soho. I talked quietly, calmly, hesitating now and then to fit in a detail. He sat back in his chair, his hands wrapped about his elbows, listening to me with a look of incredulity on his face. When I finished, he summoned the waiter and ordered two whiskeys, doubles, with no soda.

"I think you need it now," he told me as the waiter left.

"Do you think I'm insane for suspecting your cousin of—of harming Delia?" I asked.

"I don't know what to think," he replied. "It's incredible."

"I know. One just doesn't vanish into thin air nowadays. It's not done."

"Not in real life. It's all very well in books, but there has to be a logical reason for it when it actually happens. We can't afford to jump to conclusions. We have to talk this thing out, look at it from every angle."

"I've tried. If you knew Delia—"

"Don't rush me. I need to think about it for a while."

We were silent until the waiter returned with the drinks. A splotch of soft blue light fell over one side of the table, a splotch of yellow at my feet. The colors swayed with the wind, moving like live things as the oak boughs groaned. Music from the main room drifted out on the terrace, soft and muted. Alex Tanner sat with his shoulders hunched up. He fingered the knot in his tie, a deep frown creasing his brows. When the drinks arrived, he downed his in three gulps. I took a tentative sip of my own.

"This is the second time in twenty-four hours I've had alcohol," I remarked. "I hate to spoil your illusion of a worldly sophisticate, but I really don't drink."

"Finish it anyway. You need it."

I finished the drink. It was terribly strong. Alex Tanner tapped on the tabletop, still frowning. I could feel the warmth of the liquor surging through me. It made everything temporarily hazy, but I was no longer tense. I had handed my problem to him, neatly tied with a bow, and it was out of my hands. I felt a curious relief. I knew he would help me. I was no longer in this alone.

"You don't get along with Derek Hawke, do you?" I asked.

"I hate his guts, as a matter of fact, but that's no reason for me to think him guilty of a heinous crime."

"Do you think him capable of it?"

"Derek is capable of anything. But, tell me about your cousin. I know she's an actress, but what kind of person is she?"

"Vivacious. She loves a good time—a *clean* good time. She doesn't drink or smoke, although she does have a rather coarse vocabulary—like a sailor, in fact —but that's all part of Delia. She'll do anything on a dare. She once climbed up on the bronze fountain in the center of Piccadilly Circus and tossed candy kisses to the crowd that gathered around to watch. Of course, her agent put her up to it and it got in the paper with a flattering snapshot and helped enhance her reputation as a madcap music-hall performer. Madcap—that describes Delia, but she's real and warm and thoughtful and kind as well. I've seen her empty her purse for a group of urchins and cry real tears because she didn't have more. We shared the flat in Chelsea all these years. We could have moved to much grander quarters, but neither of us is very grand. She—she's just not the kind of person to run off with some man."

"I see," he replied. "I believe you."

"I believe that man has done something to her," I said. My voice trembled, and I looked away from him.

"I—I don't know," Alex said. "Everything seems to point to it, but there's no apparent motive."

"There has to be one," I told him. "There must be."

"You said your cousin drew her savings out of the bank?"

"Eleven hundred pounds. Why—why do you ask?"

"I was just wondering." His voice was very serious. He seemed to find it hard to express what was on his mind. "Derek has investments in London. A firm handles them for him. I know he's been speculating rather heavily of late, and I know he asked Andy to lend him the money to cover some loss. I haven't got any of the details, but I know she refused to give him the money. They quarreled about it. Still—that isn't important."

"It gives him a motive," I insisted.

"Eleven hundred pounds? It's not likely, Deborah."

"A man like that—"

"We've got to be fair," he replied calmly. "He claims he's never met your cousin. That could be true, you know. She could have seen the article and made the whole thing up, just as he suggested. Perhaps there isn't a man involved at all. Perhaps she merely wanted to get away for a while. The entertainment world must be frantic and nerve-wracking. Perhaps she wanted to get away from it for a few weeks without telling anyone where she was going. Perhaps she wanted to think things out, organize her life. That's very fashionable at the moment. Gurus—"

"Delia would go stark raving mad if she had to be alone for twenty-four consecutive hours," I said, "and her life was perfectly organized. She had a good job with a revue that was doing big box office, and she was perfectly contented. The idea of her consulting a guru is laughable, to say the least. They'd both have screaming nervous breakdowns."

"Yet she quit her job," he persisted.

"Because she intended to get married. She would never have done it if she didn't have a valid reason. She loved the revue."

"You can never be sure about other people," he replied.

"Your cousin said something like that."

"It's true, nevertheless."

Alex was silent for a while. He seemed to be lost in thought. The Japanese lanterns poured their colors down on the terrace. I noticed a few acorns scattered over the wooden planks, fallen from the oak trees. I could smell the river. The alcohol was beginning to hit me hard now, and everything grew a little hazy. I studied the man across the table from me. The sport coat hung loosely from his broad shoulders. His hands rested on the edge of the table, strong brown hands that seemed to have a personality of their own.

"I shouldn't have bothered you with all this," I said. "I shouldn't have brought you into it. He's your cousin . . ."

"You need help," Alex replied. "I can't believe anything is seriously wrong—I'm sure your cousin will turn up—but I can understand your distress. You can't just sit by idly and wait for her to come back home."

"I don't intend to," I said. "I intend to get proof. That's why I am staying at Blackcrest."

"I'm not at all sure I approve of that," he told me. "Why?"

"I can't bring myself to believe that Derek is involved, but if he *is*, and he knows you suspect him, Blackcrest can't be a very safe place for you. Damn! That sounds like a line from one of my books! But it's true."

"I can take care of myself."

"Look, Derek said he had a man in London working on it. Maybe he'll turn something up."

"I don't believe there *is* a man in London," I replied. "I believe he made that up to pacify me and keep me from going to the police."

"I wonder . . . I have a friend, Martin Craig. He's a detective. He's helped me several times with my books—checking details of police procedure, verifying facts about criminal behavior, and so forth. I

could put in a call to London and ask him to look into
the matter. Martin is very good. If there has been
some kind of foul play, he'll find out. He owes me a
favor. I'll call him."

"That's very kind of you."

"In the meantime, I wish you'd change your mind
about staying at Blackcrest. It makes me uneasy."

"Don't be," I retorted. "I'm a big girl now."

Alex Tanner smiled. "I'll take your word for it," he
said. "You're remarkable, you know. I've never met
anyone quite like you. Here I am, driving along,
minding my own business, leading a perfectly ordi-
nary and unspectacular life, and I stop to change a
flat tire on a rainy night and find myself caught up in
something utterly fantastic." He shook his head and
summoned the waiter. "I can't believe any of this.
Check, please, waiter."

He settled the bill, left a large tip, and led me across
the wooden floor of the terrace and through the main
room. I walked unsteadily, my head reeling a little
with the sudden motion. Alex noticed this. When we
stepped outside, he took my hand and led me away
from the parking lot and down a path that went toward the river. I did not protest. His hand gripped
mine firmly, and I stumbled once or twice. The smells
of the river were strong, crushed milkweed and moss,
mud and sulfur. It was chilly. My shoulders trembled.
Alex stopped, took off his sport coat, and draped it
around my shoulders.

"You really *aren't* used to liquor, are you?"

"I told you I don't drink. Am I drunk?"

"Not quite. All you need is a little fresh air to clear
your head. I thought you were going to fall flat on
your face in the restaurant."

"It was a strong drink," I protested.

"You're full of surprises," he remarked.

"Where are we going?"

"I thought we'd stroll by the river for a while until you're steady on your feet. There's a park of sorts down here, delightful view of the local teen-agers. They all come here to neck."

"Is that what you had in mind?" I asked foggily.

He laughed softly. "I'm no cad. I don't get my ladies drunk and then take undue advantage. However, if you've a mind to . . ."

"We'll walk," I replied. "I'm not *that* drunk."

He laughed again. It was such a pleasant sound. My arm was in his. The heavy sport coat hung on my shoulders. It was scratchy and smelled of sweat and leather, masculine. We didn't talk for a while. We walked down to the edge of the river and followed a path through the trees. The moonlight was bright, and silver filtered through the limbs. Dark purple shadows danced across the path. We crushed acorns and dead leaves underfoot. We passed a couple of startled teen-agers who were sitting on an old marble bench beneath one of the trees. The river lapped noisily at the banks. An owl hooted. It was all foggy and dreamlike, and I felt more relaxed and at ease than I had since the moment I had first arrived in Hawkestown.

Alex walked with long, loose strides. I had to take short, hurried steps to keep up with him. He led me to a bench near the edge of the water. He took my shoulders and set me on the bench as though I were an invalid who couldn't manage it alone. I leaned back against the trunk of the oak tree and closed my eyes. Alex gathered up a handful of pebbles and tossed them into the water. There was a series of soft plops as the stones skimmed the surface.

I don't know how long it was before I opened my eyes again. My head was clear, although there was a slight throbbing that I feared would be a major headache later on. Alex was standing beside the bench, his arms folded across his chest, looking down at me. For a moment I thought he was Derek Hawke. They did look remarkably alike.

"Feel better?" he asked.

"Much."

"Head clear?"

"Almost."

"Fine."

"You must think me terribly naïve, not being able to hold one glass of whiskey without staggering. I feel very foolish."

"I find it charming," he replied. "What shall we talk about? It's a lovely night. The crickets are chirping, and the moon is high, and you don't want to neck. We may as well talk."

"Tell me about yourself," I said. "I know you do a wonderful job of changing flat tires, and I know you write mystery novels, but I don't know anything else."

"Andy didn't tell you anything?"

"I'm afraid she was a little prejudiced."

He chuckled. "She's a grand old girl. I'm very fond of her, and she's fond of me, too, deep down. If I had half a chance, I could win her over completely, but there's not much point in that, is there? Derek has pretty well convinced her that I'm unworthy of notice. I should care about that, but I don't. He's willing to live his life sheltered in that old pile of stone, waiting for the money, and someday he'll get it and real-

ize the best days are over and the money isn't much
good to him. I'm content to be an outsider, a Tanner,
son of the outrageous Tanners who lived high and
died worn out and had no regrets. They disgraced the
family, but they lived. I've got no roots, no strings,
and I'm open to any suggestions."

"Are you really so nonchalant?" I asked.

"What do you mean?"

"Does Blackcrest and the family really mean so little to you? Are you really content to thumb your nose
at them and stand back and see Derek inherit everything? Isn't it as much yours as his?"

"That's Andy's decision. She's made it—with Derek's help. I'm not complaining."

"You're human," I said. "Surely you must feel *some*
bitterness."

"Bitterness? Life's too short."

"It doesn't seem fair of Andy to cut you out like
that."

"Perhaps it's not, but I guess I'm an incorrigible
black sheep. I just missed out. Derek was always the
fair-haired boy in the family. He was always proper
and good and respectful and ingratiating, even when
we were children. I broke windowpanes and put
frogs in the maid's bed and refused to eat my cereal,
while Derek behaved himself and addressed old Stephen Hawke as 'Sir' and let Andy fuss over him. Both
of us stayed at Blackcrest a lot of the time when we
were growing up. Derek knew even then that he stood
to gain by such conduct. I never gave a damn. Still
don't."

"Was he really such a good little boy?"

"When adults were around he was. He did exactly
what they told him to do. When they weren't around,

it was quite different. I was punished many a time for misdeeds he'd done. They never asked me if I was guilty or not. They just whammed away, knowing that dear Derek would never put sugar in the gas tank of the Rolls or slash Andy's best dress. He used to smirk when I'd come in with a smarting bottom. He used to taunt me—tell me that Blackcrest would be his and I'd be left out in the cold one day when we grew up."

"That's dreadful," I exclaimed.

He chuckled again. "It sounds like something straight out of *Wuthering Heights*, doesn't it? Only I'm not the Heathcliffe type. I had the fun, Derek had the rewards. It evens out."

"You don't resent him getting the rewards?"

Alex shrugged his shoulders. "I haven't got time to brood about it. Life's too full, too fun. I have all sorts of adventures. I even meet beautiful girls who have flat tires in the middle of rainstorms and need me to help them find missing relatives. Who am I to complain? Do you think you can stand up?"

"I'll try," I said.

I did. I managed beautifully.

"Steady?"

"Very."

"You're the first modern girl I've met who can't hold her liquor. I find most girls can drink me under the table. I'll bet you don't smoke, either."

"I don't."

"Remarkable. You're *full* of virtues."

"Is that bad?"

"Well . . . it's refreshing. Rather discouraging, though."

"Don't give up entirely," I said.

"I don't intend to," he said with mock solemnity.

"Much as I hate it, I suppose we'd better be getting back now," I said.

"You ready?"

I nodded, and he took my hand. We walked slowly along the path back toward the parking lot. Neither of us spoke. Alex seemed to be lost in thought. I felt comfortable, secure, knowing he was beside me. We reached the parking lot, and I took the coat off and gave it back to him. He slipped it on and adjusted the hang across his broad shoulders. We were standing beside my car. It looked terribly battered beside his ultramodern sport car.

"When will I see you again?" he asked. "We'd better keep in touch."

"I intend to drive into Hawkestown tomorrow afternoon," I said.

"Stop by my cottage. Perhaps something will have turned up."

He gave me directions. We stood beside the car, neither of us wanting to say good night. Alex scuffled the gravel under the toe of his shoe. Moonlight gleamed on the parking lot, empty but for our cars. The restaurant was dark now, the colored lights extinguished. I could hear the wind rustling the tall grasses at the edge of the river. Alex wanted to say something, I felt, but he was finding it hard to express.

"Uh—you'll be careful at Blackcrest, won't you?" he finally said.

"Very careful."

"Just in case—" he said.

"Just in case. It's been a nice evening. I feel so much better—about everything. You'll call your detective friend?"

"First thing in the morning."

"I hope he'll be able to find out something."

"He'll probably learn that she's perfectly all right, taking a rest in some resort town. I'm sure she'll turn up. I'm anxious to meet her. I have a lot to thank her for."

"Oh?"

"If it hadn't been for Delia, I wouldn't have met you. I like her already for bringing us together."

I smiled. I opened my car door. "I'd better leave now. It's been so nice . . ."

"I'm going to follow you back in my car. Can't have you going all that way alone. I'll follow you to the main gates."

"That's very kind of you, but—"

"I don't intend to argue," he replied firmly. "I feel responsible for you." He paused and looked into my eyes. Then he grinned. "It's a great feeling," he said.

9

I pulled my car in beside the old Rolls-Royce and cut off the motor. The garage was enormous, and enormously cluttered. Besides four cars, there were wooden crates and discarded furniture, and strangely enough, an old carriage with broken shafts. I got out of the car, wishing I had thought to bring a flashlight. It was very dark in here, with only a few rays of moonlight spilling in through the one open garage door. I could smell grease and oil and rust and rotting leather. My footsteps sounded very noisy as I made my way out and pulled the garage door down. It creaked as it slid down and closed with a dull thud. I stood shivering, wondering what direction to take to get to my room.

Betty had given me a key to a back door, along with specific directions on how to get back to the tower room. The door opened on a hallway that would carry me to the tiny flight of backstairs leading up to the corridor outside my room. This way, Betty in-

formed me, I would not have to go through the basement and up the winding tower stairs. I had been
dressing for my dinner engagement and had not paid
much attention. Now I was bewildered. Morris had
brought my car to the front of the house, so I had not
come out Betty's back way. I wondered how I was
going to find the door she had described to me.

The garage was in back of Blackcrest and to one
side. A flagstone path wound past dark clumps of
shrubbery and arrived at a small clearing where the
kitchen gardens began. Blackcrest rose in towering
levels here in back, ugly stone piled upon ugly stone,
flat dark windows peering at me as I walked hesitantly past the shrubbery. The house seemed to tilt a
little, and I had the strange feeling that it was going to
topple over. I walked past a row of basement windows. Several of the panes were broken, making
great jagged holes in the glass. I saw the tool shed, a
hoe leaning against the brick wall. I moved around a
corner, fully expecting to find the door. Instead, I
found myself staring in bewilderment at a high stone
fence covered with espaliered shrubs.

Had Betty mentioned anything about a fence? I
tried to remember. I recalled something about a rusty
gate. Yes, she had told me to find the gate. Then I
would pass under a series of arched trellises which
would bring me out immediately behind the kitchens.
I moved along the wall in search of the gate. The
leaves of the shrubbery rattled noisily. A cat stalked
along the top of the fence. It leaped in front of me. I
let out a cry of terror. My heart pounded violently.

This is absurd, I told myself. I was shivering with
cold, and although I tried to convince myself I was
perfectly calm, I had almost had heart failure when

the cat leaped. I felt weak, and my head throbbed. I had to stand still for a moment and pull myself together. The cat was at my feet, purring. It curled a long tail around my ankle. It took a tremendous amount of willpower to refrain from screaming again.

"Don't do that, kitty," I said nastily.

The cat, offended, stalked away. I finally summoned enough courage to move on down along the fence. The gate was set inside the deep wall, its wrought-iron pickets crusted with rust. I unfastened it and pushed it open. The hinges creaked alarmingly. I had to stoop over in order to pass through the small opening. My hand trembled as I fastened the gate back. I whispered silent curses against one cat in particular and made unflattering remarks about the whole feline species.

The high, arched trellises made a long, twisting tunnel. Honeysuckle vines grew in thick walls on either side of the flagstone pathway, and long tendrils trailed down from the wooden network overhead. Moonlight seeped in through the leaves and gilded the flagstones with a misty blue sheen. The leaves cast dancing shadows at my feet, and the fragrance was stifling. There were small stone benches at regularly spaced intervals, a straw hat and a pair of shears on one of them. The sound of my heels tapping on the flagstones echoed up and down the tunnel. The sound was upsetting. I was tense, braced for another cat to leap out at me. The wind blowing through the honeysuckle vines made a noise like whispers. I contemplated whistling a happy tune but decided against it. I could see the end of the tunnel ahead.

I had almost reached it when a loud roar split the

air. It soared for a moment and then died down to a muffled putting sound. Someone had just driven into the garage on a motorcycle. At least it sounded like a motorcycle. I could hear loud footsteps pounding on the walk along the stone fence, and a rasping screech as the gate was pulled open. I stepped into a tiny alcove behind one of the stone benches, moving quickly and instinctively. Tendrils of honeysuckle dripped down about my shoulders. I was completely in shadow, and I felt sure no one coming down the tunnel could see me. I heard the loud footsteps moving on the flagstones, strong, determined steps that came nearer and nearer.

It was Neil, wearing the black pants and leather jacket he had worn the first time I had seen him. He moved quickly through the patches of moonlight and shadow, his boots hitting the walk angrily. I felt foolish cowering there in hiding, but it would be far more embarrassing to step out now and let him see me. He moved past without glancing in my direction, but as he came to the end of the tunnel he hesitated for a moment and looked back. He seemed like a dangerous young animal, standing only a few yards away from me, silhouetted by the moonlight. I felt sure he couldn't see me, yet I could feel those fierce eyes sweeping over me. He hesitated for a moment longer, peering into the shadows where I stood, then walked on, disappearing into the yard.

I was shaken, and for some reason I felt guilty. I was a grown woman, and yet I cowered in shadows and held my breath and screamed like a bloody idiot when a cat leaped at me. I prided myself on my iron nerves, but they had certainly deserted me tonight. Here I was acting like the silliest female in the most ludicrous of early Hitchcock films. I scolded myself and walked resolutely out of the trellis tunnel. Neil was nowhere in sight. I was thankful for that.

Blackcrest cast heavy shadows over the yard, and several gigantic trees grew beyond the back steps. I could see the crumbling tower pointing like a broken finger at the dark gray sky. A light burned dimly over a small door to the side of the kitchens. I was sure it was the door my key fit. It was half a city block away, and I walked through the darkness toward it, stepping around the tree trunks and silently praising Betty for leaving the light on. I was halfway there when the light went out. I stopped, startled. The door opened, and someone stepped out onto the tiny flight of stairs. I could see the white blur of a dress, and as I peered closer, the silky sheen of platinum hair. Honora paused for a moment and then moved silently down the stairs and into the yard.

I stood beneath the hanging boughs of an oak tree, watching her. It was after midnight. Neil must have been coming home from his job at the station, and Honora must have been waiting for him. The fact that Derek Hawke had forbidden her to see the boy would mean nothing to her. I saw her gliding through the shadows, the white skirt flashing like iridescent wings as the moonlight touched it. She went into the formal gardens, passing the pond with cracked white fountain, passing the clumps of evergreen trees, and stopped by an arbor near the edge of the lake. Neil stepped out of the shadows to meet her, and the soft white splotch merged with the tall black form, too far away for me to see clearly. I sighed deeply.

How wonderful it would be to be seventeen and in love and fighting opposition and full of wild, romantic dreams, I thought. Then I remembered being seventeen and decided that twenty-four was a far better age, all romantic dreams long since dissolved and replaced by a most sensible caution. I shook these thoughts out of my head and hurried on into the house.

A light was burning in the hall, and I found the narrow stairs and went up them to the corridor that led to the tower room. The house was silent. The walls seemed to be listening to my footsteps as I went down the shabby corridor to the door of my room. Betty had left a lamp burning, and the bedclothes were turned back, a nightgown draped across my pillow. A small gas stove was burning low, and there was even a plate of cookies and a glass of milk sitting on the bedside table. I smiled as I saw the milk and cookies. Evidently I had won Betty over completely. The round room was snug and warm and seemed to be waiting for me.

I put the nightgown aside and slipped into a pair of vivid pink-and-orange silk lounging pajamas, frivolous things that nevertheless worked wonders for the morale when one was alone in a strange place. The bed was warm, the clean, coarse linen sheets smelling of soap, and I wasn't at all surprised to find a hot-water bottle tucked into the bedclothes at the foot. I sat up, propping the pillows behind my back, and reached for the milk and a cookie. Crumbs be damned, this was the kind of luxury I seldom indulged in. I must remember to thank Betty properly when she came to wake me up in the morning.

I was exhausted, so exhausted my bones ached, but I wasn't at all sleepy. I was wide awake. I could hear the wind whistling through the cracks in the wall that protected the staircase. It did indeed sound as though someone were creeping up the steps, but I was firmly resolved not to let the normal sounds of the old house bother me. Floors would creak, windows would rattle, mice would no doubt play in the walls, but I intended to ignore the noises. The room was comfortable, the bed was divine, and the milk and chocolate cookies were delicious.

I thought about Alex Tanner. I felt so much better now that I knew he was on my side. He had agreed with me that I couldn't go to the police with things the way they were, but he would put his friend in London on the case, and in the meantime I could try to find some proof that Delia had been here. Derek Hawke had denied it, and neither Andrea nor Betty had given any indications that they knew anything about it. If she had come here, it had been in secrecy. Still, someone might have noticed something, someone might suspect. Getting the job as secretary to Andrea Hawke had been a great stroke of luck. It would give me the perfect base to work from.

I reached for the last cookie. Chocolate crumbs were sprinkled all over the sheets, but I didn't care. I sat back against the pillows, reflecting. It seemed impossible that it was only yesterday morning that I had awakened in my flat in Chelsea, listening to the traffic noises outside the window and facing a long, dreary, jobless day. Had it been such a short time ago that I had sat curled up on the sofa with a cup of coffee, staring at the photograph of Delia and deciding on impulse to drive to Hawkestown? It seemed years ago. I brushed the cookie crumbs off the bed, knowing sleep would be impossible for a while.

I had brought one of Alex Tanner's books up to the

room with me. It was on the bedside table now, a thing called *With Morgue in Mind*, the title picked out in bright blood red against a garishly colored background. I took it up and turned to the first page. It was surprisingly good. Alex had a wry way of expressing himself, and the story moved along in a series of violent shocks, body piling upon bloody body, suspense mounting as the slightly dim-witted heroine went to meet the killer at a dilapidated old cottage by the seashore.

I read for almost an hour, telling myself that this was not at all the kind of thing one should read in an isolated tower room, yet unable to keep from turning the pages. At first I was hardly aware of the sound outside. I thought it was the wind. I put the book down, giving all my attention to the sound. Someone was coming up the winding stairs. There could be no doubt about it. I heard the footsteps clearly, heard whoever it was stumbling on the landing outside my door. I could not remember if I had locked the door or not. My blood ran cold, truly cold, and I was ready to let out a piercing scream when the timid knock sounded on the door.

At first I could do nothing. I sat in the bed with my heart pounding. The knock sounded again, louder this time. The doorknob turned, rattled, but the door was locked. I tried to call out, but no sound would come.

"Miss Lane?"

"Who—who is it?"

"Honora."

"My God," I said.

"What did you say?"

"Just a minute," I called.

I slipped on a pair of high-heeled pink mules and went to the door. Honora was standing there with a very pale face. I noticed grass stains on her skirt. Drafts of cold air swirled in from the landing. I pulled her into the room and closed the door, making sure that it was securely locked.

"I'm sorry to have disturbed you," she said quietly.

"I've aged ten years in the past three minutes," I replied, not in a pleasant voice.

"Did I frighten you?"

"That's hardly the word for it."

"I'm sorry," she repeated.

I started to make another sarcastic remark, when I noticed her pale face again. The girl looked shaken and distressed. I bit back the sarcastic words and forgot all about my own fright. I pointed to the overstuffed chair and told her to sit down.

"Is something wrong?" I asked.

"I . . . I don't know."

"I suppose this is just a friendly call. After all, it's only one-thirty in the morning. I'm delighted to see you. I'd offer you something, but I've already eaten the milk and cookies Betty left."

Honora perched on the edge of the chair, her hands in her lap.

"What did you want?" I asked in softer tones.

"Nothing. I was just going to my room."

"By way of the staircase and my bedroom?"

"Yes," she replied.

"Do you want to explain that?"

"My bedroom is right down the hall," Honora said. "It's away from all the others. I . . . I wanted it that way. I can reach it by coming in by the kitchen and going down the hall and up the servants' stairs, but I

. . . I didn't want to come in that way. The only other way is to come in through the basement door, up the tower stairs, and through this bedroom. I hated to bother you, but—"

She cut herself short and stared down at her hands. She was twisting them together nervously. She tilted her head back and looked up at me. Her soft pink lips quivered, and her blue eyes were full of doubt. She wanted to confide in me, but she was hesitating. I sat down on the bed and tried to pretend that I was accustomed to people dropping in to chat in the middle of the night.

"By 'coming in,' you mean coming in from the back, don't you?" I said.

"How did you know?"

"I saw you. I also saw Neil."

"He said he thought there was someone in the trellis tunnel," Honora said.

"Me. He frightened me. I darted into the shadows. When I saw who it was, I felt like a fool and didn't want to step out."

"I was worried. I thought it might be Derek—that's why I wanted to come back to my room this way. You see, we had that terrible quarrel last night, and he's been watching me all day. I think he saw me slipping out tonight."

"And you thought he'd be waiting downstairs to confront you as you came in?"

She nodded, still twisting her hands.

"Well, we've tricked him," I replied, as though it were a rather jolly conspiracy.

"I want to thank you for not mentioning seeing me last night. He suspected where I went, of course, but if you had told him for sure, I hate to think what he might have done."

"I promised, didn't I?"

She looked at me for a long moment. She seemed to be searching for something in my face—sincerity, honesty, trustworthiness—and after a while she looked away, apparently satisfied. She relaxed, sitting back in the chair and arranging the grass-stained white skirt over her knees. I sat with one leg curled under me, my hand resting on the bedpost. The girl had a desperate need to confide in someone. I had just been elected.

"You *do* understand, don't you?" she said in a quiet voice.

"I think so. I was seventeen once. I'm not exactly in the grave right now."

"Neil needs me. I need him."

"Then you're both very lucky," I replied.

"Why can't anyone else understand that? Why do they think he's only interested in my money? I wish I didn't have a cent. I wish I were a waitress or a clerk at Woolworth's. Then everyone would say how lucky I was to have an ambitious, hard-working boy like Neil. But no, I have an inheritance, and so he's no good, a teddy boy with long hair and a motorcycle. I have to meet him in secret. I have to live on plans that might never work out."

"Why shouldn't they?" I asked.

She hesitated a moment. "Derek," she said.

"There's nothing he can do when you turn eighteen."

"You don't know him. He . . . he has ways. He'll wreck everything and say it's for my own good. He's bitter. He hates people. Just because he was disappointed and betrayed once, he thinks everyone is rotten. He refuses to believe anyone can have decent motives. He suspects everyone of being . . . foul. He has no feelings. He doesn't know how to feel."

"What happened to make him so bitter?" I asked. "A woman?"

"Yes. Several years ago. She was beautiful, the daughter of one of Hawkestown's leading families. They were engaged, and everyone said they were a perfect match. Derek was different then. He laughed. He had an interest in something besides his investments and the firm in London. I was just a child, but I can remember him whistling as he came down the stairs. They would go horseback riding and have picnics and take canoe rides down the river. Then his buddy came down from London."

"His buddy?"

"They were in the service together, stationed in South Africa. Both of them were demobbed at the same time and planned to go in business together, start their own brokerage. Then his buddy came to Hawkestown to discuss financing the project, and he met Derek's fiancée. That was all. They ran off together. The two people Derek thought most of in the world betrayed him. He was never the same again. The girl came back after a few months. She wanted to be forgiven. Derek threw her out of Blackcrest. She committed suicide. She drowned herself."

"How dreadful," I whispered.

"The people in town blamed him. They said he killed her, as surely as if he'd pushed her in the river and held her down. They hate him, all of them, and he seems to thrive on their hate. He rarely goes to Hawkestown, but when he does, he's like an ancient lord come to snub the local peasants, despising them, treating them like dirt. He feels no guilt about the death of the girl. He loved her once, but when she ran away with his best friend, he murdered all feeling he might have had."

"It must be awful to have her death on his conscience," I said.

"He doesn't. He doesn't feel anything. There was a lot of resentment in Hawkestown, a lot of confusion, even talk about revenge. The girl's brother came to Blackcrest with a riding crop. He was going to beat Derek. Derek broke his arm, and the constable couldn't do anything about it because it was self-defense. The girl's family left Hawkestown, but people still remember. People still hate him. They're still afraid of him."

"Afraid?"

"Everyone is afraid of him," she said.

I didn't say anything. Honora stared in front of her, remembering. She brushed at the grass stains with one pale hand, paying no attention to the gesture. Her blue eyes seemed to be suddenly very old, eyes that had witnessed something horrifying and didn't belong to a seventeen-year-old girl.

"Does he never leave Blackcrest?" I asked.

She shook her head. "Only on business."

"I suppose that takes him to London?"

She nodded, thinking of something else.

I had to be very careful. The girl was high-strung and nervous. If she suspected that I was pumping her for information, she would shut up tight and refuse to tell me anything more. There was a delicate balance between idle curiosity and downright prying. I had to simulate the former and avoid any indication of the latter.

"When was he last there?" I asked, smoothing down the bedclothes and not looking at her.

"Sometime last month," she replied. "He had to see about some of his investments or something. He stayed at his club, I think. It was so nice while he was away. Neil and I didn't have to sneak around. It was wonderful; but he came back, and it was worse than ever."

"How long was he in London?"

"Almost a month. He left around the middle of March and came back around the middle of April."

Delia had started talking about her new boyfriend around the middle of March, and on April 14 she had taken her savings out of the bank and left London. I wondered how he would explain away that coincidence.

"Has there been any other woman since his fiancée betrayed him?" I asked. I was tense, waiting for her answer, but she would never have known it. I brushed a lock of hair from my temple and stared at one of the windows set high in the wall.

"I . . . I'm not sure," Honora replied.

Something in her voice made me look up sharply. Honora was afraid. The planes of her cheekbones looked drawn, her eyes incredibly large. A quiver started at the corner of her lips. She twisted her hands, wringing them together, unconscious of doing so.

"I saw something," she said. Her voice was flat.

"What?"

She did not reply. She didn't seem to hear me.

"What did you see?" I asked.

A shadow seemed to pass over the girl's face. She stood up, brushing her skirt. Her hands trembled as she brushed at the grass stains. I felt my heart pounding, and it took everything I had to keep from screaming at her and demanding an answer to my question. Honora did not look at me. She brushed at the dark green stains, and I knew it was a deliberate evasion.

"You can trust me," I said quietly.

She stood up straight. She passed nervous fingers along the platinum waves and looked at me with calm blue eyes. She had composed herself now, but I could sense her tension. She held herself erect, but I felt that the least little thing would cause her to crumple. She smiled at me and tried to sound natural, but her voice betrayed her.

"I must go to my room. It's so late—thoughtless of me to keep you up like this. You've been very kind—listening to my chatter. Andy says you're going to be here for at least a week. That's nice. Nice. Forgive me for carrying on—I had to talk. I've talked too much. That isn't good. Some things—"

"Honora," I pleaded. "You didn't answer my question. What did you see? It . . . it's very important."

"Then you must ask Derek," she said.

She opened the hall door. She left abruptly, leaving the door open. As I went to close it, I saw her hurrying down the corridor, her white skirt flashing in the shadows. She disappeared, and I closed the door, weak with frustration. I leaned against the door and tried to control my impatience and disappointment.

"Damn," I said. "Oh, *damn*!"

10

The scratching sound was not loud, but it was shockingly persistent. The onyx clock on the dresser informed me that it was barely six-thirty, and only a few rays of dim yellow light dripped into the room from the slits of window set high up in the wall. I groaned and buried my face in the pillow, willing the scratching sound to disappear, but it only grew more frantic, augmented by a mewing that caused me to throw the covers back and stare at the door with fury.

I marched to the door and threw it open. I was prepared to rant and rave, but the tiny creature at my feet darted around me and made a running leap at the bed. It burrowed under the covers, a tiny mound moving under the orange counterpane. The mound gave a small quiver, grew still, and was nothing but a minute lump near the foot of the bed. I stood at the door, shivering. It had all happened in less than a minute, and I was still foggy with sleep.

I jerked the counterpane back. The kitten looked up

at me, prepared to fight. It had enormous blue-green eyes and a tiny, tiny body covered with ginger fur. Seeing no lethal weapon in my hand, it rolled over on its back, flicked a tiny pink tongue at me, and kicked four padded feet in the air, expecting, no doubt, to be scratched and played with. I was in no mood for frolics. I stared at it angrily.

"Do you realize what time it is?" I demanded. "No decent cat would dare bother a person at this hour. Besides, cats don't have blue-green eyes."

The kitten rolled over and kicked at the counterpane, delighted at the sound of my voice. I sat down on the edge of the bed. The kitten stared at me for a moment, crouching on all fours, ready to pounce. Then it made a great leap and landed on the back of my hand. It sank kitten teeth into one of my fingers. I pulled my hand away, not at all amused. The kitten scrambled into my lap and began to examine the texture of my silk pajamas with four sets of claws. I lifted it up carefully and set it aside, grumbling.

"Give a girl a break," I said. "It's hardly *dawn*."

The kitten went into a fit of ecstasy and galloped around the bed, suddenly intrigued with its tail and determined to clamp its teeth about that elusive ginger member. I gave up. I went to the wardrobe and took out my clothes, not at all elated by this feline intrusion. I decided to take the animal back downstairs and deposit it with its more sensible colleagues.

I slipped down the hall to the tiny bathroom Andrea had designated for my use, washed my face, brushed my teeth, and stared irritably at the somewhat haggard face in the shadowy mirror. The kitten was still gamboling about the bed when I returned to the tower room. I put on a russet sweater and a pair of tight brown slacks, sitting down on the bed to slip on a pair of brown sneakers. The kitten, expecting some grand outing, paused in its pursuit and regarded me with a whimsical expression. It licked one paw, then another, waiting for me to finish.

"All right, sport," I said. "Let's move."

I opened the door to the landing, and the kitten leaped off the bed and followed me out. His tiny paws made small clicking noises on the cement floor. He followed me down two flights of winding stairs, purring contentedly. The basement was cold and dark.

I found the light switch that lit the bulb hanging near the door of the cats' room. The white globe burst with radiance, throwing light on the damp walls with their rusty pipes, gleaming on the cracked floor. I saw light green fungus growing over some of the bricks and could smell the decay all around me. It wasn't yet seven o'clock. I wasn't ready for this.

"Here we go, sweetie," I said, my hand on the knob of the dark oak door. "In you go."

The door wouldn't open. It was locked. The kitten seemed to be delighted. It leaped and bounced at my feet, throwing grotesque shadows on the wall. I was puzzled.

"If the door was locked, how did you get out, kid? Have you been roaming around all night?"

The kitten looked up at me with enigmatic blue-green eyes, twitching its whiskers.

"I suppose we'd better go back upstairs. Don't think you're getting off scot-free. I shall certainly report you to Andrea, and I'll personally see to it that you're punished. I could have slept for at least another hour."

The kitten was off. It ran down the long hall with

great bounds. I saw it disappear into the shadows and could hear the soft echoes made by its padded feet. I was tempted to give the whole thing up, but I felt a certain responsibility for the disreputable little creature and I didn't want it to get lost, even though there had been moments earlier when the idea would have enchanted me.

I hurried down the hall after it, leaving the lighted area behind. The hall grew narrow, until it became nothing more than a small passage. The ceiling seemed to slant down. I could hear the kitten ahead padding happily along in the darkness. There was a loud clatter as it knocked a box over. The noise seemed to explode in the silence, and the echoes reverberated against the close walls.

I passed through a room piled high with old magazines and boxes and bins. There was just enough light streaming through a basement window for me to see a rat perched on one of the boxes. I shuddered and hurried on, following the noise of the kitten. I was in the main hall again. I could feel drafts of chilly air coming through a broken window. The kitten had disappeared, and there was now no noise to follow.

I paused. There was almost total darkness here, and the air was clammy. The ceiling was so low that I almost touched it with the top of my head. The beams seemed to sag, and dusty particles of plaster drifted down like fine snow. I called the kitten in a pleading voice. Fingers of cold, clammy air seemed to stroke my cheeks. There was a peculiar smell I couldn't identify.

The cellar door creaked. It was standing wide open, and the drafts of air were coming up from below. I stood very still, listening. I could hear a gentle padding noise echoing up, a mere whisper of noise, and I knew the kitten had gone down. Andrea had complained about the door being open yesterday. This being the case, I wondered why it was standing wide open this morning. Either Morris had forgotten to close it after he brought the kitten up yesterday or else Jessie had been at it again, far more committed in her criminal nipping than even Andrea suspected.

My intentions were the best, but there are limits to everything. I wasn't about to go down in the cellars after the kitten. The smell alone was enough to make the idea thoroughly unsavory. I had visions of falling down the damp steps and breaking my neck, and if that didn't happen, I could see myself getting lost in the labyrinth. The kitten would just have to stay there until I could summon Morris or someone else who knew his way around down there. No, I'd done enough for one morning, I decided, and I was about to leave, when I heard the cry.

It was heart-rending. It was low and terrified. It came from far below, but it reached me with all the impact of a cannon shot. The kitten was lost, and it was afraid, and it cried out with a sound so plaintive that I was rooted to the spot. The cry echoed away, and then there was a whining noise, like crying. That did it. I had never particularly cared for cats, but only a monster could have walked away from a sound like that.

Luck was with me. Hanging on a bent nail just inside the door was a long, slender flashlight. I pushed the button on the handle, and a strong ray of white light penetrated the darkness. I pointed it down the steps and moved slowly down, staying near the wall. The steps were slabs of flat rock, rough-hewn and none too smooth. They were coated with moisture. There was no railing, and it was a sheer drop from the exposed side of the steps to the earthen floor below. I was thankful my sneakers had good crepe soles.

This first room was enormous and pitch-dark. The flashlight shone on towering racks that had once held bottles. All were empty now. Spiders had been at work, covering the racks with glittering silken webs. I touched one of them accidentally and shuddered as I pulled the sticky mess away from my hand. In one corner there was a broken barrel. It had once held ale. The swollen wooden pieces reeked of it. The floor was littered with empty bottles, some broken, some still containing drops of wine. I stumbled over the rough floor, pointing the ray of light here and there, calling to the kitten in a soft voice.

Several dark passages led away from this main room, and I followed one of them, stooping down so that I wouldn't crack my head on the ceiling. The passage twisted around a corner and led into a room similar to the first. Here some of the racks still held bottles of wine, row upon row of the finest vintage, all of them draped with cobwebs. There was no sign of the kitten.

I called again. I heard a scurrying sound from one of the passages that led still farther away. I followed the sound. The beam of light pointed through a long, narrow tunnel with walls of natural rock, gleaming with greenish moisture. The room I came into was filled with wooden kegs. The faucet of one of them had been left open, and all the wine had dripped out. The alcoholic fumes were potent.

The kitten was crouched on a low table beside one

of the kegs. Its blue-green eyes were enormous in the beam of light, and its tiny body trembled violently. I moved toward it, speaking soft words. It seemed to be terrified. As I reached for it, it leaped off the table and ran around me, mewing loudly. I switched the light around in time to see its fluffy tail disappearing around the corner of another passage.

I stood beside the table, hesitating. Derek Hawke had told me that the cellars spread out underneath the whole of Blackcrest, like ancient catacombs. I had already come a long way from the hazardous stairs, and I was not certain I could find my way back. It would be so easy to get lost down here. I shuddered at the thought. No one knew I had come down to the cellars. I visualized horrified hours spent in going from room to room, trying to find a way out. If I called for help, no one would hear me. The beam of the flashlight was already growing dim. I did not know how long the battery would hold out. Without light to guide me, I might never find my way back.

All things considered, it would be best to leave now while I was halfway sure I could find my way back to the stairs and the door. The kitten wouldn't starve. I would tell Andrea immediately, and she would see to it that someone came down to rescue the animal. I didn't want to lose my way in this labyrinth of rooms. The kitten would be all right, I reasoned, and then it cried again.

I gave up all thoughts of return. I couldn't leave without the infuriating little creature. I went down the passage it had taken. It was very long, much wider than the others had been, and there were beams of strong black oak supporting the ceiling. This seemed to be some sort of main passageway.

There were several cell-like rooms with stout wooden doors on either side of the passage. Some of the doors stood open, revealing drab interiors with stone walls, and floors littered with straw. I saw strands of rusty chain dangling from one wall.

The cellars were much older than Blackcrest itself. I had learned this from typing up the first chapter of Andrea's memoirs. The cellars had been part of an old Elizabethan manor that had been destroyed, and Blackcrest had been built on its foundations. I wondered what horrors had taken place down here in centuries past, what poor souls had spent their last years chained up in those cells. There was an aura of evil here, something that had permeated the place and lingered over the centuries. It was as real as the gleaming walls, as strong as the smell of corrosion.

I was genuinely afraid for the first time. The atmosphere was oppressive, and I had an instinctive feeling that something was wrong. I could not identify the sensation, but it was there. It had nothing to do with the cells, nothing to do with the rotten straw and rusty chains. It had to do with something else, something that seemed to hang in the air like an invisible fog. The air seemed to be filled with whispers not quite audible—felt, not heard—warning me to go back.

The passage ended in an enormous cavelike room as large as a grand ballroom, the black walls carved out of solid rock and draped with cobwebs that swayed like live things in the air. It was filled with towering racks that reached almost to the top of the low ceiling, row upon row of racks with narrow aisles between them. Half of them held bottles covered with thick layers of dust, and the others were crusted with rust and hung with cobwebs. It was an eerie sight, something out of a nightmare. The flickering white beam from my flashlight swept over the scene hesitantly. The light was growing dimmer by the minute. Soon it would go out completely.

I called the kitten. I heard it scurrying down one of the narrow aisles between the rows of racks. I followed the sound. I turned a corner and went down another row. I caught a quick glimpse of the kitten as it scampered away. I hurried down the aisle, and then I hesitated. For some strange reason I did not want to go around the corner and turn into the next aisle. The silent whispers seemed to stir in the air. My flesh was cold, every fiber of my being alert and chilled. The kitten was making gentle purring noises on the other side of the rack.

For a moment I was completely captive to the strange sensations. I could not move. Terror swept over me in great waves. The hand holding the flashlight trembled, and the faint white beam danced up and down on the wall. The kitten continued to purr, a gentle sound that was far more terrifying than anything else could have been at that moment. I did not want to turn the corner. I did not want to find what I knew in my heart I would find on the other side of the rack.

I finally managed to take hold of myself. One simply didn't stumble over dead bodies in cellars. Besides, I grimly reminded myself, there would be a smell. . . . I shook the morbid thought out of my head. I put on a resolute expression and forced myself to move.

I went around the corner and up the next aisle. The tops of bottles stuck out on either side, ancient corks wedged firmly in place. One of the bottles had fallen out of its wire compartment and lay on the floor. I almost stumbled over it. I pointed the diminishing beam of light directly ahead.

The kitten was near the end of the aisle, circling around a bright object on the floor. It did not run when it saw me approaching. It made a series of excited leaps toward me, then back to the object, as though to guide me toward the thing on the floor. My heart was pounding. My hand shook, and the light switched back and forth with a choppy motion, making the scene seem like something out of an old silent movie. The kitten grew still and looked up at me with enormous eyes. It purred softly at my feet.

I picked up the bright pink scarf. Tiny transparent sequins were scattered over the filmy silk. Delia had bought it at an exclusive shop in London. Redheads can't usually wear pink, but in a curious way this particular scarf had not clashed with her curls. It had been her favorite. She had worn it over and over again. She had worn it the day she left London to come to Hawkestown. It still had a faint scent of the expensive perfume she always wore.

I wouldn't let myself cry. The tears started to fill my eyes, but I forced them back. I couldn't give way now. I would lose everything I had so far accomplished. Hysteria threatened to overcome me, and I almost gave way to it. I dropped the flashlight. It clattered noisily on the floor. The kitten screeched. The light flickered wildly for a moment and then held. I leaned against the rack, my eyes closed. My head swam with dark black waves that pressed on my brain, but I held on.

Several minutes passed. I was breathing heavily. I picked up the flashlight. I moved as one in a trance would move. I hid the scarf under my sweater and lifted the kitten up in my arms. It rested its head on my shoulder, purring contentedly. I moved out of the large room and went down the passage with the cell-like rooms. Somehow or other I found my way back to the stairs. The flashlight gave a final burst of light and then went out.

I climbed the dangerous steps in darkness. I felt along the wall. I found the bent nail where the flash-light had been hanging and hung it back up. The door creaked as I pushed it open and stepped into the hall. I closed it behind me and set the kitten down. It scampered away toward the tower. I leaned against the door, trying to overcome the dizziness that suddenly possessed me.

I mastered my emotions. I tried to be cool and logi-cal, and after a while I succeeded. I went down the hall and back up to my room. The kitten followed me. It was barely seven-thirty. Hardly an hour had gone by since I first woke up. It seemed I had spent an eternity in the cellars. I was calm now.

I folded the scarf carefully and hid it in the ward-robe. It was tangible proof that Delia had been here, but it was not enough. Derek Hawke could say that I had planted the scarf in the cellars myself, and there would be no way to prove he was lying. I needed more evidence. I was determined to find it.

Betty came into the room, surprised to find that I was awake. She brought a tray with coffeepot and sweet roll. The aroma of the coffee was like ambrosia to me. Betty chatted merrily as she made the bed and straightened up the room. I found that I could speak in a level, normal voice. The coffee and conversation helped me to restore my equilibrium. Before Betty left, I had even laughed at one of her remarks.

At nine o'clock I joined Andrea Hawke in the study. She had brought up a stack of newspapers and a pair of scissors. She clipped various articles and pasted them in a scrapbook; then she proceeded to work all the crossword puzzles, occasionally asking me to help her with a particularly difficult word. I typed page after page of manuscript, and the work was exactly what I needed. It was soon twelve-thirty and time to go down for lunch.

I told Andrea I planned to go into town this afternoon and would have lunch there. We needed a new typewriter ribbon and some more carbon paper, but that was just the excuse I used to justify the trip. I had other things to do in Hawkestown. Andrea fondly handled the new pages of manuscript and said I had done enough work for the day, then asked me to pick up a new pot of glue. "And a few new thrillers from the rental library," she said, hastily explaining that they were for Jessie. I knew she intended to read them herself. I smiled.

I went to my room to change. I was glad to have gotten out of joining the others for lunch. I didn't think I could have faced Derek Hawke, knowing what I knew now. The vagrant kitten was still in my room, fast asleep in the large chair. It seemed to have adopted me. I stroked the ginger fur for a moment, and the kitten purred in its sleep. I sat down on the edge of my bed, weary, yet eager to get on with my investigation. I had made quite a lot of progress. I knew now that Delia had come to Blackcrest with Derek Hawke. Now all I had to do was establish proof of it and force Hawke to reveal what he had done with my cousin.

II

I stepped out the back door and went down the short flight of steps. It was after one o'clock, and the sun was high. It poured dazzling light over the yard. The oak trees spread heavy purple shadows over the green grass. I walked beneath the groaning boughs and entered the tunnel of honeysuckle vines. Here it was cool, the leaves rustling. I could hear bees buzzing drowsily among the blossoms. My heels made a loud rapping noise on the flagstones.

I pushed open the rusty gate, passed through the small opening, and walked along the stone fence. I had taken a long shower and changed into a white linen dress with large green polka dots. I wore a thin white straw band in my hair, and my white straw purse had a green silk scarf dangling from its clasp. I felt fresh and revitalized, glad to be getting away from Blackcrest for the afternoon.

I turned a corner and walked along the bow of broken basement windows. Blackcrest did not seem formidable in the sunshine, only old and tottering. The huge gray stones were dusty. The vegetable gardens were shabby. I walked along the flagstone path, musing, and then I saw Derek Hawke and another man standing beside the stone toolshed. Hawke was talking angrily in a low voice, and although I could not distinguish the words, I could feel the vigorous rage behind them.

The other man had graying hair and a tanned, leathery face. A pair of faded gray overalls covered his short, muscular body, and his strong brown hand rested on the end of a garden hoe. His face was passive. He listened to Hawke without flinching, but his black eyes showed pain. I knew that he must be Neil's father.

Hawke slammed his fist into the palm of his other hand and tossed his head. His voice rose. I caught the word "outrage" as I moved on down the path. I was thankful that the shrubs soon concealed me from the two men. I hurried on toward the garage, eager to be gone.

I had opened the garage door and was taking my keys out of my purse when I heard footsteps behind me. I tensed. I knew who it would be. I turned around, trying to remain cool and calm. Derek Hawke came toward me with long, leisurely strides. He was wearing brown boots, piped brown pants, and a dark green corduroy jacket with leather patches at the elbows. His white shirt was open at the throat, and the wind had blown his dark hair into a tangled mass over his forehead.

"Leaving us, Miss Lane?" he asked.

"Temporarily. I have errands."

"I was sorry you couldn't join us for lunch today. I

half-expected you to come down to breakfast, too, though I suppose you working girls like to sleep as late as possible."

"Betty brought coffee to my room," I said.

"You've made quite a hit with her, it seems. Special service. You have a way with you that wins people over—first Andy, now Betty. It is a formidable gift. Be careful not to abuse it."

"What do you mean by that, Mr. Hawke?"

"Just a word of advice," he said.

He shrugged his shoulders and gave me a boyish smile. For a moment I thought he was very like his cousin Alex, and then I noticed that his dark eyes were not smiling at all. They were examining me closely, as though evaluating competition. I remained very calm, my chin tilted up and my eyes meeting his with cool disdain.

"Perhaps you'll be able to join us for dinner tonight," he said in a deep, husky voice. "Your presence would grace any table." The stilted compliment sounded sincere. The smile that accompanied it was warm. He could be an accomplished actor, I thought.

"Perhaps I will," I said.

"I'd like that."

"Would you?"

"We decided to be friends," he said. "Remember? We decided you were not a blackmailer and I was not a villain. I had rather hoped we'd get to know each other better."

I made no reply. He jammed his hands in his jacket pockets. There was a potent, leathery smell about him that was very appealing. He was standing very close to me, and he had an undeniable attractiveness that made me nervous. I had to remind myself what this man was, what he had done.

"It seems my cousin Alex has gotten the jump on me," he said. "Will you be seeing him this afternoon?"

"How—how did you know about that?"

"About your date with Alex last night?" He grinned. "Someone saw you together and told someone else who told someone else who told one of the maids who told Jessie who mentioned it to me this morning. Not much happens in Hawkestown, but then again, not much happens that isn't known by everyone minutes after it's happened. It's that kind of town."

"That's encouraging," I said.

He didn't stop to ponder this reply. "Have you known Alex long?"

"We're friends," I replied tersely.

"Alex is a fascinating man, a successful author, young, carefree, charming. He has too much charm for his own good. I make it a strict rule never to trust a person with too much charm. It's a rule you would be wise to adopt."

"I'm a grown woman, Mr. Hawke. I think I can decide for myself the people I can trust, as well as the people I can't."

My voice was crisp. Derek Hawke stepped back, extending his palms in a gesture of mock concern, begging my forgiveness. The exaggerated gesture irritated me. He arched one dark brow, and an amused smile played at the corner of his mouth. He was silently laughing at me, and I felt a flush burning my cheeks. I gave him a sharp nod and went into the garage, thoroughly out of sorts. I got into the car and slammed the door with unnecessary violence.

He was still standing there when I backed out of

the garage. It was necessary to turn the car around before I could drive around the house, and although there was plenty of space in front of the garage, I found it difficult to manipulate the car with someone watching me. I could see him through the windshield, his hands in his pockets, his shoulders hunched forward, an amused expression on his face. It was a full five minutes before I had the car pointing in the right direction. By that time I was furious. I must have left several yards of rubber marks on the crushed-shell drive as I zoomed out of his sight.

I was still trembling with rage as I passed through the great stone portals and turned onto the main road. I was driving too fast, and the worn tires rumbled over the bumpy road. I took a deep breath, trying to calm down. It wouldn't do to let myself vent my emotions in this childish way. Through his mockery Derek Hawke had scored a point and caused me to lose my composure. He had won an easy victory, and I was irritated with myself for giving way. I eased my foot on the gas pedal and slowed to a decent speed.

This was the first time I had driven this road in daylight, and the trees and shrubbery that had seemed so foreboding at night were now sun-spangled and lovely—tall pines, giant oaks, and maples with leaves of a dozen different shades of green, from darkest green to a pale, translucent jade almost yellow in the sunlight. I passed a field of waving brown grass, brown and golden sunflowers rising up on sticky stalks to meet the sun. Behind a low gray stone fence I saw a grassy slope scattered with rich blue wildflowers, a line of silver birch trees growing in the distance. Accustomed as I was to the congested pavements of London, this rugged, unkempt beauty had a soothing effect on me, and I soon banished my ill temper.

I passed the station with pale blue petrol pumps. Without the garish lighting, it looked sordid and dilapidated, plaster flaking off the walls, the parking area littered with candy wrappers and bottle tops. I wondered if Neil were already there. I hadn't seen him in the gardens with his father. I drove through another wooded area and soon entered Hawkestown proper. It was calm and picturesque, the old houses standing serenely behind neat gardens, the oak trees making patterns of shadow over the sun-speckled sidewalks, the river winding like a sparkling blue ribbon beneath the ancient stone bridges. I drove along the main street and found a parking place across from the square. Several old men were sitting on the benches beneath the tarnished bronze statue, and groups of pigeons waddled at their feet, looking for crumbs. I locked the car and walked along the row of shops.

I strolled casually, lingering to look in a window, enjoying the feeling of freedom. Several people were shopping or just walking beneath the oak boughs: a stout woman in tweeds with a pair of binoculars slung around her neck, an old man leading a Yorkshire terrier on a red leather leash, a girl with long, tangled blond hair who wore the briefest miniskirt. Everyone I passed studiously ignored me, and I had the strange sensation that I might be invisible. At the same time, I knew that every detail of my dress and manner was duly noted. I could almost hear myself being discussed later on by these people who didn't appear to see me. Hawkestown was inbred, self-sustaining, and strangers were out of place. That was in my favor. Surely if Delia had been here there would be someone who remembered her.

The shops all had pink or gray brick fronts with large display windows. The brick was faded, and the windows were dusty. Several shops had ancient, handpainted wooden signs swinging over their doors; a few had tattered awnings. I had the feeling I was wandering across a stage set of an English village, the atmosphere mellow. After the crowded furor of London streets, this serene tranquillity didn't seem quite real. I peered through the window of an antique shop. A marmalade cat slept peacefully on a Hepplewhite chair with tapestry-covered bottom, reflected in the dusty glass of a Venetian mirror. A set of gorgeous milk-glass dishes was piled carelessly beside one leg of the chair. Such treasures hadn't yet been plundered by the commercial buyers of London, I thought. This in itself told me a great deal about Hawkestown's isolation.

I went into the stationery shop to buy carbon paper and a new typewriter ribbon. The clerk had to hunt for both items, clearly not used to selling such unconventional wares. To soothe his distress I bought a box of heavy creamy writing paper and a pot of glue. While he wrapped them all up in a neat brown parcel, I examined the pens and cards and bottles of bright-colored ink. Not once during this transaction did the clerk look at me directly, although I felt I was under serious scrutiny from the moment I entered the shop.

I was hungry, and I needed to sit down and think about exactly what I intended to do. Across the street I saw the Tea Shoppe. Unlike the other shops, it had a front of honey-colored brick, with neat green-and-white-striped awnings over the windows on either side of the green door. The final "pe" on the sign seemed pretentious, but at least there wasn't a "Ye Olde" in front. I crossed the street and went inside. A tiny brass bell jangled as I closed the door behind me.

It was cool and dim inside. The walls were soft blue, the carpet thick and gray. There were several small tables covered with snowy white linen cloths, a bowl of blue larkspurs in the center of each. I could see the gleam of fine china and silver and hear the tinkle of glass. The atmosphere was extremely genteel, soothing. I sat down at one of the tables and looked around. The stout woman in tweeds I had seen earlier sat in one corner, stuffing down tiny glazed cakes and discussing bird-watching with a thin, limp woman who sipped her tea daintily. They were the only other customers, and neither had looked up as I came in.

I was beginning to think no one would wait on me, when the back door swung open and the waitress sauntered toward me. The atmosphere of gentility was shattered immediately. This creature belonged behind the bar of a rowdy pub, selling beer and ale. She was certainly not suited for an establishment such as this. She wore a bright red blouse and a tight black skirt. Cheap five-and-ten bangle bracelets clattered at her wrists, and golden hoops dangled from her ears. Her short curls were dyed an improbable shade of black.

"What'll it be, ducks?" she said breezily.

She stood beside the table, chewing a wad of gum. Her face might have been pretty, but it was coated with makeup, the lipstick too red, the Pancake too thick, the mascara too dark and improperly applied.

Her lids were coated with blue-gray shadow, and a black satin beauty mark was stuck on her cheek. She spoke pure cockney. I wanted to ask her if she were for real, but good breeding forbade.

"Could you bring me a menu?" I asked.

"Could do," she said, "but it wouldn't do you no good. You can have cucumber-and-watercress sandwiches, tea and cakes. That's it."

"Cucumber and watercress?" I said.

"Very refined," she said. "On white bread, with the edges trimmed. Tiny little things." She seemed to think it a grand joke. She grinned impishly and wrinkled her nose at me. "You want the works? 'Course, if you're really hungry, you can go to Benton's down the block. They'll give you meat and boiled potatoes."

"I'll take the works," I said after only a moment's hesitation.

"Righto, ducks. Be right with you."

She left my table and went over to speak to the women in the corner of the room. They looked horrified when she asked if everything was all right. The stout woman paused with cake halfway to her mouth, looking at the waitress as though the girl had leprosy. The waitress laughed and sauntered on into the back. The women finished quickly, dumped a pile of coins on the table, and left. The bell jangled angrily as they slammed the door behind them.

I smiled to myself. Despite her makeup and ill-advised clothes, the waitress had that breezy, devil-may-care manner that I always found delightful. I wondered what she was doing in a place like this, and then I remembered Andrea mentioning "that awful Tottie" and saying she didn't come to the Tea Shoppe anymore since the girl had arrived. Andrea had also mentioned that Alex Tanner had been seeing the girl.

I asked myself what Alex, with all his poise and polish, could find attractive in such a girl, and I answered myself almost before the question was properly framed. He would admire that same breezy quality I had already noticed, and the girl obviously had an availability that would be most welcome in a dull town like this. The makeup and junk jewelry that offended me would only make her more appealing to a man who wanted a casual companion for an evening at home. I had few illusions on the subject. Alex was a man, and men demanded satisfaction. That was the reason for good-natured creatures like Tottie.

She came back into the room, bearing a heavily laden tray. She set it on the table, whipped off the white cloth covering the food, and displayed a plate of tiny sandwiches, a silver pot of tea, and three minute glazed cakes with pink-and-white frosting.

"Here you are, duckie," she said, pouring tea into a white cup.

She went over to the table where the women had been and scooped up the money. She rang it up on the cash register beside the door and then began to clear the table. She hummed merrily to herself as she worked. I found the food surprisingly delicious. The sandwiches were crisp and full of flavor, the tea strong and aromatic. I was eating the last cake when Tottie came back to my table.

"More tea?" she asked.

"Please," I replied.

She went to fetch a fresh pot of tea, and when she came back I was sitting with my chair pushed away from the table, completely relaxed. I smiled at the girl as she poured the tea.

"Are you a native of Hawkestown?" I asked.

"You've got to be kiddin', duckie. Do I look like one?"

"Well—hardly. No offense," I hastily added.

"None taken. You ain't either, sweets. A native, I mean. No one in this town dresses like that. The minute I laid eyes on you, I said to myself, that little number ain't from this town, not by a long shot. You stand out like a sore thumb. I mean that nice-like."

"Thank you," I replied.

"London?"

I nodded.

"Me, too, though not from the same circles, I'd wager. No, I was out of work, and the old man who runs this place needed a girl. He was in London and talkin' to a friend of his who's a friend of mine, so they got together an' fixed it up for me to come work here. Me, sellin' cucumber sandwiches! The owner almost dropped his teeth when I came sashayin' in a few weeks ago. He didn't know what to expect, but he sure didn't expect me. Nice old coot, though. Pays a decent salary, and hasn't fired me yet."

"You've been here only a few weeks?"

"Six or seven. Long enough to know this ain't the town for me. The women who were just in here, for example. Bird-watching! I ask you, is that sane? Everyone here seems to be livin' in the past. You'd hardly know it was the twentieth century. No action. Well—" She hesitated a moment, then smiled. "Almost none," she said.

"Alex Tanner?" I said.

"How'dja know?"

"Someone mentioned it."

"That's another thing. Everyone knows what everyone else is doin'. A guy gets a new stamp for his stamp collection, and the next day everyone in town knows how much it cost, where it came from, and what page in the album he stuck it. Makes me nervous—not that I've got anything to hide. I mean, Alex an' I're just friends, in case you wondered. He's a knockout, real smooth, but not my type. I like the beefy kind, truck drivers an' that sort. Alex an' I have a few laughs now and then, an' God knows he's the only person in this town who can keep a girl amused."

She put a hand on her hip and stared at me with twinkling eyes. She was engagingly frank, delightfully straightforward. Tottie was clearly a girl who loved a good time and didn't mean to be bothered by hypocritical niceties. Without makeup, jewelry, and cockney accent, she would be ideal, but I supposed they were all part of her personality.

"Just passin' through, ducks?" she asked.

"No, I have a job here."

"Well, luck to you, sweetie. Dry rot begins to set in after the first couple of weeks, and on the third you start to go stir crazy. It takes guts to stay here."

"I don't intend to stay long," I remarked.

"More power to you."

I hesitated a moment. "I . . . I am on an errand, really. Perhaps you can help me."

"Anything I can do, ducks. Just ask me."

"I'm looking for a girl. My cousin. I have reason to believe she came here. She—you see, she's disappeared in a way, and I'm trying to find her."

"Run away from home?" Tottie asked.

"Not exactly. She just—left."

I didn't intend to go into detail, but I had to try everything. It was quite possible that Delia had been seen in Hawkestown. Tottie was a bright and observant girl, and she might be able to help me. She was certainly the most friendly person I had run into in town. If she hadn't seen Delia herself, she might have overheard some gossip. I told her about Delia's disappearance, leaving out everything that concerned Derek Hawke. I didn't want to bring his name into it. Not yet.

"Hey, that's too bad," Tottie said. "Imagine runnin' off like that and just vanishin', not thinkin' about you and how worried you'd be. A girl like that needs a good shakin'."

"I . . . I am afraid something has happened to her."

"Don't you believe it, duckie. Despite what you read in the papers an' all, nothin' happens to a girl that she doesn't *want* to happen. She will turn up, older an' wiser an' probably richer from the experience. I can see why you're worried, though."

"Right now I just want to find proof that she was here. If I could do that, I'm sure I could eventually locate her . . . or find out what happened to her."

"What does she look like?" Tottie asked.

I took out my purse and pulled a snapshot of Delia out of my wallet and showed it to Tottie. She studied the picture for a long time, pressing her brows together in concentration. I could tell she was trying to remember seeing Delia. After a moment she shook her head and handed the picture back to me.

" 'Fraid not, ducks. Lots of people come in here, an' I'd have remembered her. Pretty little thing, cute face an' all. No, mostly old folks come in the shop, birdwatchers and tweedy types who like to gorge on cakes and tea after shoppin' a bit in town. She never came in. What did you say her name was?"

"Delia. Delia Lane."

"Pretty name. Doesn't ring a bell, though."

"She's not too tall, and her hair is red—blazing red, cut short. I think she might have been wearing a pink scarf over her hair, and she had on a full-length gray fur coat the last time I saw her."

Tottie snapped her fingers and nodded her head rapidly two or three times. "Hey—just a minute," she said. "When did you say she was supposed to be here?"

"Around April 15. Almost six weeks ago."

"Yeah, I would've been workin' here just a few days myself. I know she never came in here—I'd of remembered for sure—but when you said that about the red hair and pink scarf, I remembered something. One day things were kinda slow here, an' I was standin' at the window an' I saw a girl go past the shop. She was walkin' real fast, and I couldn't get a real good look at her, but I remember the scarf and the red hair. It was a strange combination, I thought. Red hair and pink don't go together, but this didn't clash at all. There were little sequins on the scarf. I remember them twinklin' in the sunshine. I said to myself, that must've cost a pretty penny, that scarf. It could have been your cousin, though I wouldn't swear to it."

"I'm sure it was. I didn't mention the sequins on the scarf. You remembered that on your own. It was Delia, all right."

"Hey, that's swell. At least you know she got here safe and sound. Now we're gettin' somewhere."

She stood leaning against the table, her bracelets jangling every time she moved her hand. She wore a cheap, too sweet perfume, but at the moment it smelled heavenly to me. Tottie straightened her skirt and ran her fingers over her short black curls. She looked pleased with herself for remembering.

"What do we do now?" she asked.

"I . . . I don't know."

The bell jangled, and an old man in a brown leather jacket came into the shop. He settled at a table, coughed, and took out a huge pipe. He pulled out his tobacco pouch and began to fill the pipe as Tottie walked over to the table to take his order. She greeted him heartily, and he smiled feebly, coughed again, and ordered tea and cakes. I sat lost in thought, wondering what I should do next. There must be some logical way to go about this. I couldn't just go around canvassing the neighborhood and asking everyone I met if they had seen Delia. Then I had an idea. I wondered why I hadn't thought of it before. I took a pencil and notepad out of my purse and tore off a clean sheet. I printed the telegram Delia had sent me, word for word. I remembered it perfectly.

"What's that?" Tottie asked.

She had served the old man and was back at my table.

"It's a copy of the telegram my cousin sent to me. I'm going to go to the telegram office and see if they remember her sending it. Where is the office?"

"There isn't one. Not as such. The post office is down the block. You can send telegrams from there. Just one old woman runs the place, a crazy old character who comes in for tea now and then. Jiggs, they call her. She gives me the creeps. She sorts mail and sends telegrams, does all the work herself, though a regular man delivers the mail, of course. You can rent books there, too. It's the only library Hawkestown has, not that I spend much time readin', mind you. Old Jiggs may be able to help you."

"I'll see," I told her.

"Be careful with her—she's senile, at least when she wants to be. She lives over the post office in a tiny room, and they say she keeps two Great Danes up there, though no one's ever seen 'em. People claim they hear 'em barkin'. Of course, there's them who say Jiggs is the one barkin' at night. Creepy."

"Very," I said.

"These small towns," Tottie said, shaking her head. "You hear how weird people in *London* are. I'm here to tell you they can't hold a candle to some of the characters I've seen right here during the past six weeks."

I paid Tottie for the food and left a large tip. I thanked her for her help and walked toward the door. Tottie rang the money up on the cash register and smiled at me. She began to straighten up the stacks of chocolate mints piled in a dish beside the cash register.

"Don't you worry," she said. "Everything will work out."

Her voice was sincere. Something in her eyes told me that Tottie was genuinely concerned with my problem. She was very real, very human, not at all the outrageous creature I had first thought her. She arranged the mints in their silver dish and wrinkled her nose at me.

"You—uh—you won't mention any of this, will you?" I asked.

"Mum as mum, luv."

"Thank you again," I said. "You've been kind."

"Don't mention it, duckie. And good luck with Jiggs. I think you'll need it."

12

The post office stood on a corner. It was a narrow building two stories high, the gray brick faded. Blue curtains hung at the windows of the second story, and a flourishing green plant grew in a pot behind one of them, creating a very domestic effect. The lower story had two large, dusty plate-glass windows, POST painted in flaking gold leaf on one, OFFICE on the other. In the lower-right-hand corner of one was a tattered cardboard square with RENTAL LIBRARY printed in clumsy black block letters. The door stood wide open, and it was very dark within. I stood for a moment in the dazzling sunlight, apprehensive; then I walked into the building, the slip of paper clutched in my hand.

To my left there was a wall of mailboxes, each one with its own name tag and tiny glass door, and to my right there were several racks of books, their colored jackets protected with plastic covers. At the end of the small building there was a large wooden counter behind which a woman worked sorting mail. Her back was to me. I saw several parcels on the counter, as well as a telegraph machine, various pads and pens, two wooden trays, an ancient cash register, and a flowering cactus plant. The place smelled of dust and glue. There was an electric light behind the counter where the woman worked, but the front of the building had to rely on what little light came in through the dusty glass windows. The floorboards creaked as I walked across them. The woman did not turn to look at me. She kept on sorting mail with nimble hands, stashing the letters in various compartments with an alarming speed.

She seemed to be so frantically busy at the moment that I was loath to interrupt her. Tottie's description of Jiggs had prepared me for an eccentric, and I knew that if I intended to get any information whatsoever, I had to be very careful. I turned to the racks of books, remembering that Andrea had asked me to pick out some thrillers "for Jessie." The racks had four sides, on revolving stands, and I turned them slowly, trying to make as little noise as possible.

The books were surprisingly well read, the pages thumbed and bent, the check-out slips in front stamped profusely. I supposed the people of Hawkestown did a lot of reading in lieu of the more glamorous entertainments offered by the city. All the bestsellers were here, all the new thrillers. I chose four that looked particularly bloody, hoping Andrea would find them stimulating. I took the books back to the counter. The woman continued to sort mail, ignoring me. I coughed discreetly.

"You'll find a card in back of each book. Fill in name, date, and address. I'll do the rest later on. Advance deposit required. Leave it on the counter." Her voice was harsh and masculine.

"How much?" I asked.

"Can't you read? Says so right there on each jacket. I don't have time to read it to you! Devon, Dorset, Norfolk, Oxford, New York. New York!" The woman had been tossing letters in compartments, barely looking at them. She paused and examined the letter in her hand. "Hmm. Rae Stanton, addressed to a cosmetics firm. Probably hopes to find a cure for that acne!" She tossed the letter in a compartment marked OVERSEAS, then continued her work, chanting. "Leicester, Warwick, Oxford again, Kent—are you still there? Haven't you got the correct change?"

She turned around for the first time and stared at me as though she expected me to leap over the counter with a dagger. I stepped back, my eyes wide. The woman studied my face, her blue eyes hard and thorough in their scrutiny. I tried to smile pleasantly but failed to carry it off.

I was sure Jiggs was harmless enough, but she looked like something out of a gangster movie. She was small and wiry, with steel-gray hair cut close to her skull. Her face was a network of wrinkles, brownish with tiny purple veins. A wart protruded from the side of her nose. Her lips were thin, the corners of them stained with tobacco juice. She wore a pair of soiled blue coveralls with, strangely enough, a large pink-enamel daisy fastened to the lapel.

She studied me for a moment longer and then reached into her pocket to pull out a knife and a plug of tobacco. She cut off a generous piece and stuck it in the corner of her mouth.

"Ain't seen you before, sister," she said.

The "sister" was too much. I smiled to myself. I had studied enough basic psychology to know immediately that Jiggs was a lonely old woman who craved attention. In order to satisfy this craving, she had created a personality that would not go unnoticed. Like most eccentrics, she was deliberate and studied in her eccentricity. The plug of tobacco gave proof of that. She probably hated the stuff.

"I am Andrea Hawke's secretary. She asked me to pick up some books for her."

"Thrillers, I see! Old Andy still say they're for the cook?"

"I think they are."

"Don't you believe it! She reads 'em herself. Better than sleeping pills, she told me once. She ain't foolin' anyone."

I wanted to tell Jiggs that *she* wasn't, either, but I thought better of it. She stamped the check-out slips, stacked the books to one side, and counted my money before ringing it up on the cash register. Then she stared at me again, grimacing. I decided that flattery was the best way to reach her. If she wanted attention, I would give it to her.

"Do you do *all* the work here?" I asked in an innocent voice.

"Every lick and smack of it!"

"Amazing," I said.

"What do you mean?" she demanded, ready to take offense.

"I would think it would take three or four people," I said. "I've just been here a day or so, but I've already noticed what wonderful mail service Hawkestown has. We have nothing like it in London. You drop a letter in the box and just pray for the best."

As obvious as the tactic was, it worked. Jiggs preened visibly. She smiled smugly and nodded her head. Her blue eyes were full of satisfaction.

"Been doing it for over twenty years," she said, "day and night. Live right upstairs, and if work piles up during the day, I grab a bite to eat and then come right back down and light into it. Sort every piece of it myself, incoming, outgoing. Used to make the deliveries myself during the war, and you think *that* wasn't something. Rainstorm, snowstorm, there I was in my boots and mackintosh, heavin' that bag. People don't appreciate it." She shook her head, frowning. "No, Old Jiggs is a loony, the town character, and little children run, but they get the best mail service in the country. Why, I remember a time—"

At that point the door banged, and a man in khaki came in, saving me from a no doubt lengthy monologue. The man carried a burlap bag over his shoulder. He slung it down and leaned it against the counter, breathing heavily. His face was flushed, and he wiped drops of perspiration from his forehead. Jiggs gave him a withering glance, seized the burlap bag, and slung it behind the counter. It landed with a plop, and several letters spilled out.

"You're thirty minutes late," she snapped. "Truck break down?"

"I had to stop for a beer and sandwich."

Jiggs gave him a look that left no doubt as to what she thought of such laxity. The man was brawny and husky, but he backed away from her. She sneered as he left the building.

"Panty-waist," she said. "Ain't none of 'em nowadays got grit and gut. Don't know how to do an honest day's work. Don't understand the meanin' of the word."

"I imagine you know a lot about the people in Hawkestown," I said, smoothly changing the subject.

"The stories I could tell if I was a mind to! Ain't many secrets I ain't on to. You'd be surprised—letters, postcards, bills, magazines that don't belong in decent homes! I'm on to all of 'em."

"Are you good at remembering faces?" I asked.

"Ain't a face in this town I don't know."

"Have you ever seen this girl?" I asked, abruptly showing her the snapshot of Delia.

She took the photograph and studied it carefully. Then, apologetically, she reached into her pocket and pulled out a pair of spectacles. She studied the photograph again, squinting her eyes behind the thick glass. She took the glasses off and handed the picture back to me. She shook her head.

"I'm not sure," she said, "so many people coming, people going, me so busy half the time I don't even look up when they come in."

"She was wearing a pink scarf and a gray fur coat. She sent a telegram. This telegram."

I handed the slip of paper to her. She read it aloud.

"ECSTATIC EXCITED ELATED STOP WEDDING ARRANGEMENTS BEING MADE STOP I'LL WEAR WHITE AND ORANGE BLOSSOMS STOP IMAGINE STOP TAKE CARE STOP BE SURE TO MISS ME DARLING STOP DETAILS TO FOLLOW. " She looked up, nodding her head. "Sure, I remember her. Pretty little thing with red hair. It must have been six weeks ago—April 15 the telegram says here in the corner. Yes. That's about the time she came in. Couldn't forget anyone as striking as that. Didn't recognize the picture at first."

"You sent the telegram?"

"Sure did."

"Would you have a record of it?"

" 'Course. Right here in this ledger. Want me to check?"

"Would you?"

Jiggs whipped open the ledger, turned a few pages, and ran her finger down a column. "Here it is. Sent to London on April 15. A Miss Delia Lane to a Miss Deborah Lane, Chelsea address. That what you wanted to know?"

"Yes," I replied quietly.

"She your sister?" Jiggs asked.

"My cousin," I said.

"I suppose she ran off and eloped with some ne'er-do-well, stopped here to send you a telegram. I thought it was peculiar at the time. She came in here breezy and bright, smiling all over the place. She was all bubbly, like she'd been drinkin', only she hadn't, or I would of smelled it. I remember her well. That girl had mischief in her eyes, cute little thing, but mischievous, for all her smiles. Like it was some sort of grand lark. Never saw her again, or the man either."

"A man came in with her?" I asked, trying to contain my excitement.

"No, he didn't come in at all, and I wouldn't of noticed him if she hadn't waved at him as she left. He was in a big dark car. I didn't pay any attention to what kind it was. He was wearing sunglasses, that kind that wraps around your face like goggles, and he had dark hair. She ran and got in the car with him, slid right up against him, and they drove off."

"You . . . didn't recognize the man?"

"The car was across the street, under a tree, and I

just noticed the sunglasses and dark hair. He kept his head down, I noticed that. Could have been anyone, I suppose. Say—there's nothing wrong is there? He wasn't one of them gangsters—"

I smiled, playing it cool. "Oh, no. I just wanted to know for sure that Delia sent the telegram. She . . . she plays pranks."

"Probably told you she was goin' on a vacation, then ran off with that man. Sounds like something these young girls would do. Irresponsible, all of 'em. She'll regret it, if that's any comfort."

It was evident that Jiggs was willing to go into some detail about her opinion of the younger generation, but I gathered up the books and smiled at her, indicating my readiness to leave. She had given me more information than I had hoped for, and that tattered ledger held all the proof I needed to show that Delia had actually sent the telegram. Jiggs looked a little disappointed that I was leaving. I doubted if she often had an opportunity to talk as much as she had this afternoon.

"You say you're working for Old Andy?" she asked.

"Yes. I'm typing up her memoirs."

"She finally getting those things finished?"

I nodded, edging away from the counter.

"If they're ever published, this town's going to be gaspin'! Old Andy was a high-steppin' filly back in her day, and her husband's father was the founder of this town. There were lots of juicy scandals back in those days, and Andy didn't miss out on much. Went to school with her, I did. She was a lulu then—still is."

"Thank you very much for your help," I said, cutting her short in as pleasant a manner as possible. "Since I was in Hawkestown, I wanted to check on the telegram to satisfy my curiosity. I'll tell Mrs. Hawke you remember her."

"You do that. Tell her I might write a book myself!"

Jiggs turned back to her bags of mail, and I left the post office. I stood just outside the door, looking across the street at the oak tree the car had been under. The boughs drooped low, casting thick shade. It would have been almost impossible for Jiggs to have clearly identified anyone sitting in a car there, particularly someone wearing sunglasses, but I was certain the man had been Derek Hawke. I could visualize Delia waving at him, running across the street with a smile on her lips, getting into the car with him. The car had driven away. . . . I refused to dwell on it any longer.

I went to my own car, put the books and parcel in the back seat, and locked it again. I went back to the Tea Shoppe. The old man had gone, and Tottie was alone in the shop. She was rearranging the blue larkspurs in their white bowls, humming a song to herself. She seemed surprised to see me again so soon.

"Hello, ducks. Did you forget something?"

"No, I wanted some more information."

"Sure thing, luv. Fire away."

"I want to know about the churches of Hawkestown."

Tottie arched an eyebrow and pursed her lips. "You've come to the wrong place for that kind of information, duckie. I mean, I'd help if I could, but I haven't stepped foot in either of them."

"There are only two?"

"Righto. Catholic and Episcopal."

I frowned, thinking.

Delia's telegram had said that wedding arrangements were being made and mentioned white and orange blossoms, and that indicated a church wedding. If what she had said were true, I could safely assume that she had already discussed plans for the wedding with someone at the church, perhaps even made arrangements for the ceremony itself. She would not have been married in the Catholic church, as she was not of that faith, and that left just the Episcopal. Tottie told me a Vicar Blackstock was in charge and gave me directions for getting to the vicarage.

"Got another lead?" she asked.

"I think so."

"Jiggs was helpful?"

"Very much so."

Tottie smiled, patting her short black curls. "Good luck to you," she said. "If you need to know anything else . . ."

"Thank you again," I replied. "You've been an angel."

"First time I've ever been called *that,*" Tottie said.

13

The vicarage was only a few blocks away. I decided to walk, knowing the exercise would do me good and help curb the growing excitement I was beginning to feel. I passed the town square and turned down a shady lane with large, substantial houses set behind beautifully kept gardens. I crossed a small stone bridge and followed a footpath through the park. Bright yellow daffodils grew wild on the rich green slopes of lawn, and there were formal beds of white and yellow daisies. Birds flitted from tree to tree, chirping angrily as I walked beneath them. On the other side of the park there was a dirt road, and across the road the vicarage stood behind a low wall of gray rock. I opened the gate and stepped into the yard.

I was rather worried as to what I should say, how I should present my problem to a complete stranger. I had no intentions of telling him the complete story, and I wondered how I was going to elicit information from him without revealing my suspicions. I was over the shock of finding the scarf now, but I did not know if I could keep my composure if the vicar began to ask pointed questions. I shook these thoughts out of my head and looked up at the house.

The vicarage was constructed of the same gray rock as the wall. It was an ancient dwelling with dormer windows and a neatly thatched roof. The yard was poorly kept, just a few patches of grass, the rest dirt, but tall red and purple hollyhocks grew all along the fence inside. It was a humble, mellow place, and some of my apprehension vanished as I walked up the path and knocked on the front door. The vicar obviously had little time for gardening, I thought, and that seemed a good sign to me. I heard hurried footsteps within, and in a moment the door flew open. A rather breathless middle-aged woman stood wiping her hands on a long white apron. She smiled radiantly and nodded her head at me.

"Come right in, dear," she said, as though she had been expecting me.

Her round cheeks were flushed pink, and there was a compassionate look in her light blue eyes. She had soft brown hair turning gray, and a drab blue dress covered her plump body. Somehow she made the garment seem beautiful.

"Are you Mrs. Blackstock?" I asked.

"Yes, dear. Come . . ."

She led me into a foyer with white walls and a dark green carpet. A green vase of daffodils stood on a small white table, and a hat rack was draped with two raincoats, a black cloak, and a jaunty red cap. The woman smiled again and stood back to look at me, still wiping her hands on the apron. A delicious odor drifted in from the back regions of the house.

"You must forgive me, dear," she said. "I'm making strawberry preserves, and things are in chaos, absolute chaos. I'm afraid our maid has deserted us—poor thing, she's gone back to Liverpool—and the house is in shambles. Why I chose to make preserves at a time like this, I'll never know." She shook her head, then looked at me again with that compassionate gleam that made me feel strangely guilty. "You see, we all have problems, dear. Robert is in the library. I'll just announce you. You wait here."

She turned down a hall, and in a moment I heard her opening a door. "A young woman to see you, Robert," she called. "I'll bring her right in." She returned and took my hand, leading me down the hall. She gave my hand a gentle squeeze as we stopped in front of the door. "It'll all work out," she whispered. "Now don't you worry." I walked into the room, extremely unnerved by this curious reception. I felt like a sinner come to do penance, and that wasn't my intention at all. The man who walked toward me did little to relieve this mood.

He was tall and stoop-shouldered, with tawny gold hair tumbling in heavy locks over his large skull. His broad face was pink, dominated by an enormous nose that had been broken and gave him a rather savage look. He wore a pair of heavy horn-rimmed glasses behind which dark brown eyes glared strongly. He wore brown tweed pants and a brown-and-gold-checked hunting jacket with dark leather patches at the elbows. A pipe stuck out of one pocket, and his flowing green tie was sprinkled with ashes.

His hands were large and bony, and they seized both my own, pulling me toward him.

"There, there!" he said. "You look fine and fit. Just relax! We needn't be in any hurry about this."

His voice was gruff but kind. Vicar Blackstock gave an impression of enormous vitality and strength. With his broad shoulders and thick neck, he would have looked more at home behind a team of mules than behind a pulpit, I thought, and I was sure his sermons would be full of fire and brimstone and violent crusades against Satan. He squeezed my hands and pulled me across the room.

"Just a moment," I protested.

"Don't be nervous, child!"

"There seems to be a mistake—"

"We all make mistakes," he said firmly, leading me across the room. "We're human beings. It's comforting to know that all of us err, though hardly encouraging to men of my calling. Now, you sit down here. We're going to relax and get to know one another before we discuss anything. I understand completely—"

"I don't believe you do," I said. "You see—"

He held up his hand for silence, and furrowed his brows. There was a firm determination in his manner that would make argument futile. I gave a little sigh and delivered myself to his ministrations.

"That's better," he said in senatorial tones. "Now, we'll just finish this puzzle. It'll relax you, make things easier later on."

He sat me down at a card table on which a partially completed jigsaw puzzle was spread out. He had fit all the edges together and filled in one corner section. A formidable assortment of pieces was piled to one side of the table. "It's the Matterhorn," he said, taking a chair across from me. "I spent most of the morning on it. I find them most stimulating, most conducive to thought. Some of my very best sermons have come to me while I've been fiddling with these things. I have over a dozen of them, but the Matterhorn is my favorite. It's so majestic! Now, you take the white, I'll take the blue. Sort them all out; then we'll try to fit them together. I've been searching for a piece with a rounded edge. There's a little green sprig at one corner."

I was utterly bewildered, and trancelike, I obeyed. I gathered up all the white pieces, and in the process, found the piece the vicar had been looking for. He gave a little cry of glee, grabbed the piece, and slapped it in place as though he had a personal vendetta against it. The man had an amazing vitality, which made even something as sedentary as fitting together a jigsaw puzzle seem like a blood sport.

We worked industriously at the puzzle. The vicar seemed delighted to have someone helping, and in a short while we had the whole thing almost completed. I sat back in my chair and looked around the room. Two walls were covered with golden oak bookshelves crammed with books, magazines, and papers. A cocker spaniel with glossy brown coat was curled up on a brightly colored rag rug in front of the fireplace. The desk was cluttered with books and papers. A shabby old sofa covered with cracked brown leather stood against one wall. The room was a masculine lair, and it emanated the personality of the man who lived in it.

"There!" the vicar cried, slapping the last piece in place. "We've succeeded. Ah, Lucy. You've come at just the right time. Here, set it on the edge of the table!"

Mrs. Blackstock had come into the room with a tray holding a plate of cherry tarts, a tarnished silver teapot, and two chipped blue cups. She smiled at me and looked at the vicar with love. He treated her in a rather surly, masterful manner which I was certain delighted her. She poured the tea and waited for his next command. He unfolded his napkin and jerked his head, indicating dismissal. Lucy Blackstock left quietly, shutting the door behind her.

"Now," the vicar said abruptly. "Who is this man? I can understand your loyalty, but we have to know his name if justice is to be done. No need for you to cover up for him any longer."

I stared at him in amazement, unable to speak.

"Come, come," he said sharply. "It's a little late in the game for you to start denying anything. Ellen called me this morning. She was in tears and told me all about the sleeping pills, told me she'd manage to send you over this afternoon for a little talk."

"Ellen?" I said.

"Ellen Rogers! Your cousin. Come, child," he said irritably. "I know all about it."

"I've never met an Ellen Rogers," I replied.

"What!" he roared. I thought he was going to leap across the table at me. "You're not pregnant?"

I shook my head. "Sorry to disappoint you," I said gently.

"This is outrageous!" the vicar cried. He pushed his chair back and marched to the door. He threw it open and shouted his wife's name. She came rushing down the hall, out of breath and obviously alarmed by this sudden loud summons.

"What is the meaning of this, woman! Why didn't you tell me this young woman wasn't Ellen's cousin from Devon? Here I've been running on like a bloody idiot, making an absolute ass of myself, and all·the while she isn't pregnant at all! Explain yourself!"

"Ellen called and said her cousin was coming. I assumed—"

"You assumed!"

"Now, Robert . . ." his·wife said quietly.

"Blast it, woman!" He smashed his fist into his palm and heaved his shoulders, trying to control his anger. His wife spoke soothing words I couldn't hear, and the vicar finally sighed. He turned to me with a sheepish expression.

"I must explain," he grumbled.

"No need to," I replied. "Evidently you took me for someone else. I quite understand."

"Ellen's cousin just came to town last night, and she tried to swallow half a bottle of pills an hour after she arrived. Ellen said she'd send the girl over, and as I've never laid eyes on the cousin, I figured you were she. Please accept my apologies. Lucy's, too, I'm sure."

"I'm terribly sorry . . ." Mrs. Blackstock began.

"Go on back to your jam," the vicar snapped. "You've done enough harm for one day. Now, young woman, what did you wish to see me about?"

"My cousin," I said.

"Is *she* pregnant?"

"I certainly hope not."

The vicar looked a little disappointed. "Go on," he said.

I explained my mission briefly, merely saying that Delia was missing and that I had reason to believe she had come to see him about wedding arrangements she had wanted to make. I showed him the photograph and described what I thought she might have been wearing. The vicar nodded his head vigorously, moved quickly over to the desk, and pulled out a small desk diary. He riffled through the pages until he found the entry he was looking for.

"Did she come to see you?" I asked hopefully.

"I believe so." He frowned and flipped some more pages. "When did you say she was here?"

"Around the middle of April."

"April 15!" he said. "I jot down a line or two about everyone who comes to see me. It's so easy to forget things otherwise. Here she is! Delia Lane, she said her name was. Is that your cousin?"

I nodded, my heart pounding.

"Yes, I remember her. Charming little thing—red hair. Full of sparkle, smiled a lot. Says here she wanted me to perform the ceremony in my church during the following week. She was vague about details but said she'd come back in a day or two for definite plans. It says here Friday. She was to come back on Friday for definite arrangements. She never came back. Peculiar. I often wondered what happened to her. Did she and the fellow have a tiff?"

"I . . . I'm not sure."

"Family trouble, probably. She told me the family didn't know about the wedding yet—it was to be a surprise. Those things never work out. The man's family probably found out and raised a ruckus, thought she was after his money or something."

"Did she tell you anything about the man?"

"Wouldn't give me his name. Stubborn about that. Said she didn't want it to get out yet. From the way she talked, I gathered that he was wealthy, from one of the best families. She's missing, you say?"

"Yes. I . . . I'm a little worried."

"Probably gone off to nurse her wounds. Blow to her ego and all. Takes time to heal. Is there something I can do?"

"Not just now," I replied. "Later you might be asked to repeat what you've just told me, but I . . . I don't want to alarm anyone just yet. Delia will probably come back."

"Of course she will! Don't you worry."

"I'll try not to," I said.

I was elated with my success. Not only had the vicar remembered Delia, but he had also made an entry about her visit. It was the kind of proof I needed. He didn't press me for any details. He seemed satisfied with the little I had told him.

"You've been very helpful," I told him.

"That's my duty," he retorted.

"Thank you so much," I said, preparing to leave.

He insisted that I stay and help finish the tea and tarts. We sat back down at the card table, and the vicar talked charmingly and volubly about his work. When he mentioned the leaking church roof, I insisted on donating some money toward repairs. He took the money with alacrity and stuffed it in the pocket of his jacket. His wife was waiting for me in the foyer as I was leaving. She thrust a jar of still-warm preserves into my hands and smiled at me with her lovely blue eyes, apologizing again for her error.

I left the house and stepped into the sunshine.

As I was opening the front gate, I saw a lumpy young woman with red-rimmed eyes and stringy brown hair trudging down the dirt road toward the vicarage. She sniffled audibly and dragged her feet. I knew she must be Ellen Rogers' unfortunate cousin and hoped the poor creature would be more responsive to the vicar's ministrations than I had been.

I hurried across the dirt road and into the park, feeling exactly like a modern-day Alice just back from her sojourn in Wonderland.

14

I drove down a lane shaded with tall elm and maple trees, turning down a narrower road that ran along the edge of the river. Alex had given me specific instructions, and I soon saw his cottage standing beneath a clump of maple trees. The leaves rustled, dappling the white brick with sunlight and shadow. Neat brown shutters were fastened at all the windows, and the roof was of brown shingle, a dusty red chimney sprouting up one side. There was a pleasant air of rustic seclusion about the cottage, and I could see why Alex had chosen this place in which to write. I parked the car and got out. Alex met me at the front door.

"I've been expecting you," he said. "Have any trouble finding the place?"

"None at all. Your directions were perfectly clear."

"Fine. I've just finished my daily stint at the typewriter and am in need of stimulant. I was just about to mix a drink. Can I make one for you?"

"Not this time," I replied.

"I forgot," he said, grinning. "Can I get you something else?"

"Nothing. But you go ahead."

"I intend to," he told me.

He led me into a large, airy room with off-white walls and a bright yellow carpet. Open French windows looked out over a small, somewhat shabby garden, and I could smell the soil and hear the birds. I sat on the long tan sofa while Alex mixed his drink at the portable bar. He was silent for a moment while ice cubes tinkled against glass.

I watched him mix the drink. He wore a pair of brown slacks and a light sport coat of tan-and-brown-checked material. A vivid red tie was knotted loosely about the collar of his white shirt. The clothes were a little rumpled, as though he'd been working in them, and his hair was untidy, yet even so he had a casual elegance about him, a comfortable air that was far more appealing than bandbox neatness would have been. I had never met any other man who put me at ease so completely, to whom I warmed so immediately.

"I phoned Martin Craig first thing this morning," he said casually, coming to perch on the arm of the sofa. "He is quite interested in all this. Promised to phone me tonight if he's discovered anything. Are you sure you won't have something?" he asked, indicating his glass.

"Quite sure."

"Can't say I haven't tried to be a genial host," he replied, sipping his drink. "What do you think of this place?"

"It's enchanting."

"Hardly that. I do like it, though. Provides just the right background for a man of letters, wouldn't you say?"

"Definitely."

"I keep an apartment in London for playtime, but when I'm working, I rusticate here."

"How is your book coming along?"

"Slowly. At the moment I am more concerned with this real-life mystery you've dropped into my lap. Martin seems to think there might be something to it."

He stepped over to the bar to set the empty glass down. He folded his arms across his chest and stared at me, suddenly grim. All pleasant banter was over now. His dark brown eyes were serious.

"We talked for almost half an hour. I told him everything you told me last night, then repeated it for his tape recorder. He's in between cases right now and is going to devote all his time to finding your cousin. He'll get to the bottom of this."

"I certainly hope so."

Alex frowned. "To be perfectly honest, I didn't pay much heed to it last night. I knew you were upset, and I knew you had reason to be, but I didn't think there was anything seriously wrong. I merely assumed your cousin had decided to go off for a while without telling anyone. I certainly didn't believe my cousin Derek could be involved. I'm not so sure now."

"What made you change your mind?"

"Martin Craig. He was very interested in that angle —Derek, the money he needed to cover his losses, the money your cousin had taken out of the bank. He asked me several pertinent questions. He made it quite clear that there was a possibility your suspicions might be correct. He seemed alarmed that you were actually staying at Blackcrest."

"Really?"

"I told him I'd see to it that you left immediately. I've reserved a room for you at the hotel. I'll go to Blackcrest myself and see that your things are sent to the hotel."

"You'd better cancel that reservation," I said.

Alex shook his head slowly. "No, don't argue with me, Deborah. I've given this a lot of thought. God knows I don't want to believe that Derek is some kind of fiend—I can't accept that, I refuse to—but even if there's a remote chance he's guilty, then Blackcrest isn't safe. You have no business being there."

"I'm not leaving," I replied firmly.

"Deborah, you don't seem to realize—"

"You don't seem to realize what this means to me. Do you think I'd be able to sit in a hotel room while a man in London piddled around? I'm sure your friend is good, and I'm grateful to you for bringing him into it, but I can't just sit and hold my hands. Being at Blackcrest gives me a marvelous opportunity to work on it myself, and I've done a pretty good job of it today."

"What do you mean?"

"I found Delia's scarf in the cellars this morning."

"You went down into the cellars!"

"One of the kittens ran away. I followed it. It went down there; I went after it. It . . . it was early in the morning. No one else was up. I was afraid the kitten would get lost."

"So you risked breaking your neck, or worse. That was a foolhardy thing to do! It only goes to show how right I am, how necessary it is that you leave Black-crest."

"But I found Delia's scarf! Don't you see, I found proof that she was actually there."

"The only thing I can see right now is how obstinate you're being," he replied irritably.

"Alex," I said, "please understand—"

"I'm trying to. You're acting exactly like one of my heroines. If I'd created you on paper, I'd let you do all sorts of heroic things. I'd let you prowl along dark corridors and peer into empty rooms in the middle of the night. I'd let you set a trap for the villain and then confront him boldly with the evidence you'd gathered —but, damnit, this isn't one of my books. This is real life. You can't do things like that. What if you'd fallen down the cellar stairs? What if you'd gotten lost? What if Derek *were* guilty and had seen you go down there."

"None of those things happened," I said testily. "And I did find evidence. Delia's scarf was there on the cellar floor. It still had some of her perfume clinging to it. Don't you see what that means?"

"Deborah—"

"And that's not all. This afternoon—"

"I suppose I may as well listen to you," he said, frowning. "You seem determined to carry on with this thing. What other daring deeds do you have to relate? After you went down to the cellars, did you hide in a closet and listen to mysterious conversations? Did you—"

"Don't," I said. "Don't make fun of me, Alex."

"I'm sorry. It's just that I'm concerned. I'll listen to you. Go ahead."

I told him everything I'd learned this afternoon. He

listened with patience, his head tilted a little to one side, the frown still creasing his brow. He seemed about to interrupt me several times, but he restrained himself. When I finished, he tugged at his red tie and gave a heave of his shoulders.

"Incredible," he said.

"There can't be much doubt now," I replied. "The scarf, the entry in Jiggs's ledger, the vicar's diary— they all point to one thing. Your cousin lured Delia here with the promise of marriage, and then—"

"Enough," he said. "Let's don't jump to conclusions, Deborah. It seems that way. I'll admit that. You've done quite a job of detecting—Scotland Yard could probably use you—but you've gathered what is known as circumstantial evidence. You've verified that Delia came to Hawkestown, sent the telegram, and talked to the vicar about a wedding ceremony, but that's all. You've found no one who actually saw Derek with your cousin."

"I intend to work on that."

"No, we'll let Martin work on it. He's coming to Hawkestown tomorrow. You can talk with him yourself. You can tell him all this, and he will know what to do. He can do much more than you can. You've done all you can do."

"No, I haven't."

"What do you think you can do that Martin can't do better?" he said angrily. "He has professional skill, ways and means—"

"I have my own ways and means," I snapped. "I think I'm on to something."

"And what would that be?"

"Honora. I . . . I think the girl knows something. I think she's seen something that upset her, something she'd like to forget. Last night she almost told me about it, but . . . she was frightened. She was afraid to tell me about it."

"Afraid?"

"Terrified."

Alex seemed to be very interested. I told him about talking to the girl last night. I described the way she had acted before she left the room. He ran his thumb along his lower lip, his eyes watching me intently as I spoke.

"There might be something to it," he said, "though I doubt it. My aunt's ward is a strange girl—neurotic, high-strung, fanciful. She may have seen something, and then again she may have merely wanted attention and used those veiled hints in order to get it."

"She wasn't acting, Alex. I know that."

"Just the same—"

"I think I can win her confidence," I said. "I think I can get her to tell me what she saw. It . . . it might be what we need."

"Let's be logical about this, Deborah. Supposing Derek *had* brought your cousin to Blackcrest; don't you know he would have been careful? He would have been cautious, secretive. He wouldn't have been so clumsy as to let himself be seen. He would have done it in the dead of night—"

"Exactly," I interrupted. "That's probably when Honora saw them."

"Her room is near the tower, far away from all the others. She may be neurotic and high-strung, but she doesn't roam around the house in the middle of the night."

"But she does," I protested.

"What do you mean, she does?"

"You don't know about her romance with Neil?"

"The cook told me she had a crush on the boy. What does that have to do with this?"

"Everything. She slips out of the house to meet him when he comes home from work. I saw her running across the backyard last night. Neil was standing in the shadows, waiting for her. They stayed out there for over an hour. They've been meeting like that for a long time. She may have seen something one night as she returned to her room."

Alex nodded his head, very grim. "That puts a new light on it," he said. "This is far more serious than I thought."

"Can't you see why it's imperative that I stay? Martin Craig may be able to discover all sorts of things, but he wouldn't be able to work on it from the inside. I'm there, at the very source, and I can't leave, not until this thing is solved."

"It's dangerous, Deborah. Far too dangerous."

"I'm not afraid."

"You should be."

"Perhaps I should be. Right now I can't think of anything but finding my cousin—or finding what happened to her."

Alex came over to the sofa and looked down at me. The grim lines of his face relaxed a little, and his dark brown eyes were warm. He shook his head again and rested his hand on my shoulder. His wide mouth spread into a smile, faintly mocking.

"You're a strange creature, Deborah," he said quietly. "I've never met anyone quite like you. You're stubborn and obstinate and unyielding and full of fight. I admire that. It seems you've won. There's no way I can keep you away from Blackcrest, short of

tying you up, gagging you, and stuffing you in a
closet. I'll not resort to that—yet."

"I'm glad you see things my way."

"I don't. I'll indulge you for a little while—with reservations. You wait here. I'll be back in a moment."

He left the room. I was mystified, wondering what
he was going to do. I stepped over to the open French
windows and stared out at the shabby little garden
with its untidy flowerbeds and ragged grass. Maple
trees grew all around it, and above them the sky was
lightening, taking on that misty quality of twilight. As
the sun slipped from view, banners of apricot light
spread on the horizon, soaking into the blue and
staining it. A gentle breeze rustled through the dark
green leaves of the maples, making a soothing sound,
and I could smell all the pungent odors of the garden.

I knew that Alex was genuinely concerned with my
safety, and it was pleasant to know. His concern was
flattering. I wished that I were able to respond in the
typically feminine fashion to his concern, become
soft and yielding and leave everything to him. But he
had said I was stubborn and unyielding, and it was
true. This was something I had to do myself, and I
had a hard, cold determination to see it through, a
determination that would allow no softness, no fear.
There might be danger, but I was prepared to face it.

I was lost in thought and did not hear Alex return.
When I turned around, he was standing in the doorway, watching me with intense brown eyes. He came
toward me, and I was so caught up by the look in
those eyes that I did not notice the gun until he held it
toward me.

"Since you're determined to act like one of my heroines," he said, "you may as well have the proper equipment. Take this. Keep it with you at all times."

"Is that—a gun," I said foolishly.

"The genuine article," he replied grimly.

"But—"

"Take it," he said.

I looked down at the gun with startled eyes. It was an ugly thing, short, black, and deadly. He thrust it into my hands, and I felt a chill as the cold metal touched my flesh. It was surprisingly heavy. I held it awkwardly, as though it might explode at any moment.

"Do you know how to use it?" he asked.

"I . . . I suppose so."

"Ever used one before?"

"Not a real one. I once did *The Letter* by Somerset Maugham in repertory. In the opening scene I shot my lover. I just held the thing up and fired away, over and over again. Blanks. It made quite a noise. I kept my eyes closed—not a very convincing murderess."

"This works exactly like your stage gun, but it fires real bullets. This is the safety catch. It's locked. You just snap it back and pull the trigger, just like in the movies."

"Do you really think this is necessary?" I asked, rather nervous to be holding the vile thing.

"If you'd listen to reason, it wouldn't be."

I stepped over to the sofa, opened my purse, and dropped the gun into it. It made a plopping noise as it fell among the various feminine articles. I snapped the purse shut and wiped my hands. There was something flippant and incongruous about the gesture that made Alex grin. I stared at him with defiant eyes.

"That's that," I said.

"Be careful you don't blow your own head off with that thing."

"I think I can handle it," I replied crisply, my moment of nervous apprehension gone. "After all, I did shoot my lover night after night, for seven weeks running."

"With your eyes closed," he retorted pleasantly.

"They'll be wide open from now on," I promised.

"I certainly hope so. I mean that seriously, Deborah. Watch out. Promise me that you'll be careful and not do anything foolish. This is not a game, not a role you're playing."

"I know that, Alex. I . . . I promise to be careful. I'd better leave now. It's getting late."

"Martin is due in Hawkestown tomorrow. I'll get in touch with you. I'll call or come to Blackcrest. If you don't hear from me, don't worry about it. Martin may want to work on his own before he talks to you."

"Very well. I'll expect to hear from you tomorrow or the day after that."

"In the meantime—"

"In the meantime I'll be very, very good," I said.

He led me to the front door and out to where the car was parked. I put the now heavy purse onto the seat and got behind the steering wheel. Alex leaned against the side of the car, his arms resting on the window frame, his eyes examining my face.

"I wish I could know for sure everything will be all right," he remarked. "I wish I could know you wouldn't do anything headstrong."

"I gave you my promise," I said, taking out my keys.

"I know." He sighed heavily. "I'll be glad when this is all cleared up," he continued. "I'll be glad when we can meet as you and I and not as fellow detectives. Then we could talk about you and me and the moon and never mention Blackcrest. I look forward to that time."

"And in the meantime, there's Tottie," I replied, rather wickedly.

Alex grinned, not at all affronted. "She's a good kid," he said, "but not exactly what I had in mind for a rainy day."

"What *did* you have in mind?"

"We'll discuss that later."

He stepped away from the car and stuck his hands in the pockets of his jacket. He stood there with his head tilted to one side, the breeze fluttering the locks of dark hair and whipping his red tie up over his shoulder. I put the car in gear and backed out of the driveway. Alex lifted his hand in salute as I turned onto the main road.

It was later than I had thought. The apricot stains on the horizon had turned to dark gold, and already the air was thickening. Soon darkness would fall. I intended to have dinner with the family tonight, and I did not want to be late. I drove fast, punishing the car as I sailed over the bumpy back roads toward Blackcrest, heedless of worn tires and dubious springs. The last golden stains were fading as I turned through the large stone portals and headed down the private road that would lead me to the house. I slowed down, knowing that I had plenty of time now. Although evening shadows were fast falling, I had not turned on my headlights. Neither had the other car. I gave a violent blast on the horn as I saw it almost upon me.

Neither of us was going fast, but neither of us had seen the other. I jerked the wheel and shot the car off the road, slamming on my brakes in time to avoid crashing into a tree. The other car went on, oblivious of the near accident. I caught a quick glimpse of an aged, weathered face behind the windshield, and I knew at once that it was Neil's father. The car was piled high with luggage and boxes, and as I turned to watch it disappear down the road, I saw a gleaming black motorcycle strapped onto the back.

I pulled back onto the road, more shaken than I cared to admit. My hands were trembling as I jerked on the headlights. I drove the rest of the way to Blackcrest at a snail's pace, wondering what had happened to cause this sudden departure of the gardener with all his luggage and his son's motorcycle.

15

The house seemed to be brooding. I had noticed it when I first came in, and now as I dressed to go down to dinner I could not shake the curious sensation that something unpleasant had happened, that the very walls of the house had absorbed the ugliness and held it. There was a silence, a grim, hushed silence like that which follows a storm or some disaster. I had the feeling of suspended motion, of loud voices just hushed, of violent emotions banked down and smoldering.

I thought at first that my imagination was playing tricks on me. I had had a trying day. My nerves had been frayed and my emotions had run the gamut, but I was cool and calm now. No, this sensation did not come from within. It hung over Blackcrest like a pall. Something unpleasant had happened, and the atmosphere was permeated with its aftereffects. I dressed slowly, frowning a little, wondering what I would find when I went down to join the others.

During my absence, Betty had pressed the dress I intended to wear. It hung in front of the wardrobe now, a sober black with a high neck, a tight-fitting waist, and a short, flared skirt. The material was somewhat shiny with age, but the expensive simplicity of the garment still had an enduring chic. I slipped into it, smoothing it down about my waist and tugging at the freshly pressed folds of the skirt. I fastened on a wide leopard-skin belt, then emptied the contents of my purse into the small leopard-skin bag that matched the belt. The gun made a slight bulge, but I didn't want to leave it lying around the room for one of the servants to discover.

It was almost eight o'clock when I left the room. I walked slowly around the maze of hallways that would eventually bring me to the staircase that led down to the main hallway. Only a few lamps were burning, giving the barest minimum of light, leaving the rest of the area shrouded in shadows. The curious silence still prevailed. It was almost as though Blackcrest were holding its breath, waiting for another eruption of violent emotion.

When I reached the head of the staircase, I paused for a moment to stand among the dusty green leaves of the potted plants. I could hear voices now, coming from the small drawing room beside the dining room. Although I could not distinguish individual words, there was no mistaking that harsh, guttural voice that soared up so forcefully. Derek Hawke was angry again. I wondered who the victim of his wrath was this time.

I hesitated, not wanting to go down, yet knowing that I must. I had already lost some of my confidence at the very sound of that voice. Despite my determination, I did not know if I could face Derek Hawke and keep control of my emotions. I was afraid I would fly at his face with claws unsheathed, or worse, dissolve into tears of hysteria and demand immediate answers to the questions that plagued me. It would take all my training as an actress to go through with this with the poise I knew I must maintain.

I took several deep breaths and started down the stairs. I was halfway down when Derek Hawke stepped into the hall. He stood at the foot of the stairs, watching me. He was glowering, his mouth surly, one brow arched arrogantly. I managed to keep complete command of myself. I gave him a cool glance and continued on down the stairs.

He stood with his hand resting on the banister. He was wearing a pair of black slacks, cut close to the leg, and a rather flamboyant jacket of maroon broadcloth embroidered with black silk floral designs. The jacket would have been effeminate on many men, but on Derek Hawke it only served to offset his rugged masculinity. There was a row of tiny ruffles on his gleaming white shirt front, and the maroon silk bow tie was knotted carelessly. He looked like a pirate dressed by a mod tailor, and the effect was one most men would have paid dearly to achieve. He wore the clothes as nonchalantly as he would have worn a bathrobe.

"I see you've managed to join us, Miss Lane," he said in a mocking voice. "All dressed for the occasion, too, I see. We're not at our best this evening, but perhaps you can bring a bit of levity."

"I'll try to," I said, and I was surprised at how calm and normal my voice sounded.

"Did you have a nice afternoon?" he asked.

"It was quite profitable."

"I'm pleased. You missed quite a lot of excitement here. I seem to be a dastardly villain. Not only do I thwart true love, but I overstep my authority and undermine my aunt's position."

"How perfectly dreadful of you," I remarked.

"I'm catching it from all sides tonight. Perhaps you will be kind. Perhaps you'll be on my side—though I doubt it. You're a woman. Women are incurably romantic. You'll undoubtedly think me vile, too."

"Perhaps I shall. Would you really care what I thought?"

He looked up at me with his dark eyes. For a moment it was almost as though he genuinely wanted my sympathy, my understanding, and then his wide mouth tightened into a frown, and that moment was lost.

"Frankly, not a bit," he replied.

He took my hand to help me down the last two steps. There was something arrogant and mocking in the gesture. He released my hand and stood back to examine me again. I was as cool and poised as a mannequin as his eyes swept over me, but I could feel that poise slipping.

"Do I meet with your approval?" I asked icily.

"Very much so."

"Are you always so rude?"

"You dislike being admired?"

"I dislike being stared at, Mr. Hawke."

He grinned wickedly, pleased that he had irritated me. "It seems I am a monster," he said. "Rudeness is the least of my crimes. You must bear with me. Are you sure you want to go through with this?" he added in a grim voice.

"I'm not sure I know what you mean."

"These formal dinners of Andy's are always a pain. She was brought up in that era when one always dressed for dinner, and I endure them to please her. As I mentioned, we're not at our best tonight. There's been a family crisis—they're becoming all too frequent—and I don't think it will be especially pleasant for you to sit through. I can have Jessie prepare a tray for you."

"I wouldn't think of it," I said.

He seemed about to say something more but restrained himself with a visible effort. He turned his back on me and walked back into the drawing room, moving in quick, angry strides. I followed him, feeling not the least bit of trepidation.

Andrea Hawke stood in front of the pearl-gray draperies. She gave me a preoccupied nod and then glanced at her nephew with a perplexed expression. She wore a floor-length gown of royal purple velvet with long, elegant sleeves. Although the gown was old, the nap shiny, it was still a regal garment, and Andrea wore it with all the flair and confidence of a true grande dame. She toyed with a long black fan, and I could sense her tension. The air was electric with it.

"She still hasn't come down yet?" Derek Hawke snapped.

"Not yet, dear."

"I'll give her five more minutes!"

"Derek—"

He glared at her, and Andrea bit back whatever she had been about to say. The tension seemed to crackle. Derek Hawke stalked about the room, one hand jammed in his jacket pocket, the other tugging at the maroon tie. He was like a panther, the anger and energy charging through him and making it impossible for him to stand still.

"I so wanted everything to be nice for Miss Lane—" Andrea began.

"I told her there'd been a family crisis. She didn't have to join us. Since she has, she may as well see us as we really are. I'll put on these damn clothes once a week and eat from the best china and crystal, but I'll be damned if I'll stand around and make polite chit-chat when I feel like cracking someone's skull!"

I gave him a caustic glance. Andrea Hawke drew herself up.

"You seem to forget you're in my house," she said.

"Oh, to hell with your house," he barked. "I indulge your whims, and I overlook your maddening conduct, but I have no intentions of letting this place become a brothel."

"Really, dear—"

"I warned her I wouldn't put up with it, but she kept right on seeing him, sneaking around at all hours of the night like a promiscuous little slut. I told Jake what was going on, and I told him to keep his son away from her, but he didn't seem to be able to. He knew what a good thing it would have been if that boy could have trapped her. He'll have second thoughts now."

"Jake has been with this family for over twenty years. What will he do now?"

"I haven't the foggiest idea, and I couldn't care less."

"You could have at least let me speak to him, Derek."

"It's over and done with, Andy! Now maybe that girl will listen to reason. Five minutes are up!"

He marched over to the wall and pulled a cord, jerking it savagely. In a moment Morris stepped into the room. His uniform was spotless, his silver hair brushed sleekly, but his withered old face looked as though it might crumple at any moment. The servants must have been discussing the affair all day below-stairs, and I wagered there wasn't a one of them who wasn't on Honora's side.

"Go fetch Miss Honora," Derek Hawke commanded. "Tell her she is to be down here in ten min-utes or I'll be up after her myself."

"Leave the girl alone," Andrea protested.

"Hurry up, Morris!" he said sharply.

The butler left the room, and Andrea Hawke frowned, her eyes growing cloudy. She toyed with her black fan, slapping it against the palm of her hand. "I just can't believe it," she mumbled. "I just can't be-lieve it's happening." She shook her head and seemed to drift off into her own private fog, her blue eyes distressed. "My own nephew . . ." she whispered.

"I'm sorry, Andy," Derek Hawke said impatiently. "I haven't meant to hurt you."

"I can take it," she said. "I'm old, and I don't matter. It's the girl—"

"I've only done what's best for her."

"She said she loved him."

"She's a child. She's not capable of seeing him for what he is. He would ruin her."

"Even so, you don't have to torment her now. Why can't you let her be? Do you have to force her to come down here?"

"I won't let her sulk and brood. She's got to face

things. She has to accept reality. She thinks I'm a monster now, but the day will come when she'll thank me."

"I wonder," Andrea Hawke said. "I wonder. . . ."

She turned her back on us. She parted the pearl-gray draperies and stared out at the night. There was a flash of lightning, and from far off came the rumble of thunder. Derek Hawke stared at his aunt, and his eyes were dark. A painful frown creased his brow, and he looked as if he wanted to go to her and beg her forgiveness. For a moment he was vulnerable, exposed, and then he saw that I was watching him. I knew that both of them had forgotten my presence in their emotional stress.

"I told you it wouldn't be pleasant," he said.

I made no reply. A sarcastic smile formed on his wide mouth.

"Sorry we couldn't provide witty Noël Coward dialogue."

"The situation hardly calls for it," I said.

"You have no idea what the situation is," he told me.

"I think I can guess."

"No, you can't. You know nothing about it. The gardener's son has been courting Honora. The girl is young, foolish, vulnerable. He's only interested in her money—and she'll come into quite a lot of that in a few months. I warned the boy's father to keep them apart. I talked to him again this afternoon, just as you were leaving, as a matter of fact. He said he'd do all he could, and then the boy had the audacity to storm into my study this afternoon and tell me that he and Honora were going to be married, that there was nothing I could do about it. I proved him wrong. I threw him out and gave him and his father till sundown to be off the place."

"How very proud you must feel," I said.

I was unable to keep the hatred from my voice. I stared at the man in his elegant clothes as though he were Satan himself, and Hawke seemed almost pleased at the intensity of my stare. He arched a dark brow and tugged at the maroon tie, the mocking smile never leaving his lips. He started to make some remark, but before he could begin, Honora came into the room, startling us both.

"Good evening," she said. "I'm sorry if I've kept you waiting. I knew Andy wanted us to dress for the occasion. It took a little time." She smiled at me and nodded at Derek Hawke. Her voice was as cool and pleasant as a crystal stream, and her poise was exquisite. I knew what agony it must have cost her.

She wore a yellow dress the color of buttercups. The skirt swirled about her knees, and the bodice displayed her young figure to advantage. Her platinum hair was coiled and curled to perfection, a yellow ribbon fastened at the back. Her lips were coral, and if she had been crying, the skillfully applied eye makeup revealed no evidence of it. There was something odd about her, I thought, something that had not been there before. It took me a while to realize what it was.

The soft, poignantly fragile quality seemed to have vanished from her face. In its place was something hard and frighteningly mature. It was something I recognized instinctively, and I knew it was not just the strain, not just the hard-imposed poise. I was looking at a woman who has been hurt and is bent on revenge. The metamorphosis was alarming. There was steellike control as she looked up at Derek Hawke, challenging him with her lovely blue eyes.

"Are we all ready?" she asked pleasantly.

Derek Hawke was wary, totally unprepared for this reaction. I could sense his uneasiness. He would have known how to deal with a wretched, teary-eyed teenager, but he was completely at a loss with this strange new Honora. He frowned and shifted nervously, looking at her with lowered brows. Honora knew she had disturbed him, and a faint smile played on her lips as she went over to Andrea and took her guardian's arm.

We went into the dining room. The meal began in silence. I tried to concentrate on the bowl of consommé but found it impossible. I could not even pretend to eat. There was too much tension in the room. Morris removed the soup bowls and brought in the filet of sole. As he left, he cast a furtive glance at Honora, apparently as bewildered by her poise as Derek Hawke had been.

The draperies across the great sweep of windows were opened, and I could look out at the terrace, illuminated now by flashes of lightning. Thunder still rumbled in the distance, coming closer and closer. We were in for a storm. It was building up slowly, but it would surely explode with savage fury. Here, inside the dimly lighted dining room with its gleaming mahogany and cut glass and blue-gray wallpaper, another storm was brewing, and I feared it would be even more violent than the one outside.

Honora had made her entrance with perfect control, creating exactly the reactions she had hoped for, but the victory was short-lived. Derek Hawke had gotten over his first uneasiness and he was now in command of the situation. He made casual remarks, apparently relaxed and at ease, and seemed to be enjoying the situation. Andrea was still in her fog, only looking up from her plate occasionally to cast bewildered looks at her nephew. The strain was beginning to show on Honora's face, and she was fast losing that first remarkable poise.

Derek Hawke made no references to this afternoon's drama. He talked about the approaching storm, about Andrea's memoirs, about a political meeting to be held in Hawkestown. He did not seem to be at all perturbed that no one replied to any of his comments. A smile flickered on his lips, and his eyes never left Honora. I could see what he was trying to do. He intended to break her down, to shatter her poise and make her react accordingly. Then he could handle her. Then he would have the upper hand again.

I toyed with the fillet in my plate, pushing bits of fish around in the butter sauce. I wondered how long this could go on. I was ready to scream myself, and I knew that Honora could not hold up much longer. She was, after all, only seventeen, and remarkable transformations at that age are of short duration.

"So," he said, "that about covers it. Are you interested in politics, Miss Lane?"

It was a direct question. I had to answer.

"Not passionately," I said.

"Most women aren't. They're only interested in the private little worlds they've fabricated for themselves after reading too many novels and watching too many soap operas on television. Most of them are incapable of seeing life in its true perspective—particularly those who are extremely young."

He paused dramatically and stared at Honora. She raised her eyes to meet his stare. Her lower lip quivered slightly.

"I think I'll ask to be excused," she said.

"Oh? Aren't you feeling well?"

"You're a complete bastard, Derek."

He was delighted with the insult. "Is that one of the words your friend taught you? Apparently I was right about his bad influence. What else did he teach you?"

"Derek," Andrea warned, coming out of her daze. "This has gone far enough. Honora, dear, he didn't mean—"

Honora ignored her guardian and spoke directly to Hawke.

"I'm not going to talk about Neil with you. You'd love to see me cry, wouldn't you? You'd love to see me beg you to bring him back. I'm not going to give you that satisfaction."

"Just what *do* you intend to do?" he asked casually.

"You'll find out soon enough," she whispered.

She stood up abruptly. She flung her hand out and knocked over a glass of dark red wine. Threads of the liquid splattered over her skirt, looking like streaks of blood. Honora looked at me, and there was something imploring in her eyes. She hurried from the room. I laid my napkin on the table, excused myself, and went after her.

She was standing at the foot of the staircase, waiting for me. Her face was pale, and her blue eyes looked enormous. Now that she was away from Derek, she no longer had to pretend. She was breathing heavily. Her hand trembled as she brushed at the red stains on her skirt, succeeding only in smearing them worse.

"I—I hoped you'd come," she said. Her voice sounded frantic.

"I thought you might need me."

"There is something I must tell you—"

Her words broke off as a loud clap of thunder sounded outside. It was like a mine explosion, and the very foundations of the house seemed to shake. The lights overhead flickered, dimmed. Honora started. She seized my hand.

"He's a monster," she said. "I—I'm not afraid of him any longer. I won't let him get away with this. I won't keep quiet. I have to tell someone. You'll listen, won't you? You'll—"

The thunder sounded again. The lights grew even dimmer. Honora's face was in shadow.

"The cellars . . ." she whispered hoarsely. "Six weeks ago. We were planning to meet there. It was cold, too cold for the gardens. I got there early . . ."

She looked over my shoulder. Her hand tightened on mine. "Tonight in my room," she said quickly. "After everyone is asleep. I'll wait—you must come—"

She released my hand and rushed up the stairs. I turned around to see Derek Hawke approaching. His face was grim. I wondered how much he had heard. I was trembling. I wanted to rush after the girl. I stood in place, watching him, knowing I couldn't take much more. If he so much as spoke to me I would fly apart, lose complete control.

The thunder rumbled. The window frames rattled. The lights flickered out, and there was a moment of complete darkness before the dim yellow glow spread again. Derek Hawke stood directly in front of me. His face was inches from mine. He seized my arms.

"What nonsense has she been saying?" he demanded. "Tell me!"

"You're foul—" I whispered. "Let me go!"

"Take hold of yourself! You've got to understand. I know it seems monstrous, but you must see—"

I tried to break free, but his hands merely tightened their grip. I shook my head, refusing to look into his eyes. I knew I was hysterical. I knew all my carefully planned composure was shot to hell, but I could not control myself. In another moment I would be screaming. He swung me around into his arms. His lips bore down on mine, and there was nothing but sensation, sharp, violent sensation that crushed me under its merciless impact.

Derek Hawke released me abruptly. He stood back. A dark lock of hair had fallen across his forehead, and he shook it back. His eyes spoke volubly, but his wide lips remained stretched in a single tight line. He stood looking at me while crashes of thunder deafened both of us. I was panting, and my eyes were filled with smarting tears. Derek Hawke turned around and walked back down the hall, leaving me standing there alone, a victim of my own raging emotions.

16

The clock in my room had stopped. I had no idea what time it was. I did not know how long I had stayed there on the bed, fighting to control the conflicting emotions that shattered me. Miraculously enough, I had fallen asleep. I sat up now, rubbing my eyes. The dress Betty had ironed so skillfully was now a mass of wrinkles, and I could see by looking into the mirror that my face was flushed, my hair tangled. I took my brush and began to work on the long russet waves. The motion was soothing. I brushed vigorously, listening to the rain pounding outside. The storm was at full force now.

I felt better. My head still throbbed a little, but I was in control of my emotions once again. Perhaps hysteria had been good for me. I had given way. I had unleashed all those feelings that had been banked down for so long, and now, purged, I was, if anything, clearer and more determined than ever. I put the brush aside and tried to smooth out some of the wrinkles in my skirt. Honora would be waiting for me. I had to handle her with care, and I did not want to go to her looking like a wraith.

I needed to apply just a touch of lipstick. It was in my bag. The bag was not on my dresser. I looked about the room. I had been trembling when I came in, and I wondered where I had tossed the bag in my distress. It wasn't on the nightstand. It wasn't on the chair. I stopped cold. I remembered setting it on a table in the drawing room. I had not picked it up when I left. It must still be there, that telling bulge showing to anyone who might glance at it.

My Lord, I thought, what if he's already seen it? What if he's already opened it and discovered the gun? I had to get it immediately. I couldn't let it sit there all night. I cursed myself for my carelessness. Alex had been right. I wasn't suited for this at all. There was nothing I could do now but go down after the bag and hope no one had already discovered it, hope that no one would see me as I went down to retrieve it.

I stood in the middle of the room for a moment, debating. Alex had mockingly compared me to one of his heroines, and he had mentioned wandering down dark corridors and hiding in closets. I had no intentions of hiding in closets, but I would have to move stealthily down several dark corridors, just like one of those dim-witted creatures he spoke so disparagingly of. How he would laugh if he could see me now. Well, to hell with it, I thought. He needn't know. I would simply go down and get the bag and keep quiet about my own foolishness.

The clock had stopped at nine. That was lovely. I didn't know if it was ten in the evening or three in the morning. I didn't think I had slept for long, but I couldn't be sure. Everyone might be asleep, or the servants might still be up, checking on the windows and seeing that the storm did no damage. If I went along the maze of corridors and down the main stair-case, I would surely run into someone. It would be safer to go down the tower stairs, through the base-ment, and along the side corridor with all the win-dows. That would bring me close to the drawing room and I would be much less likely to meet any-one. I might have been insane enough to forget the bag, but at least I was shrewd enough now to think out the best way of getting it back without being seen.

It was chilly on the landing. The rain was pounding furiously outside, and great waves of it lashed against the walls as I made my way down the winding stair-case. There was complete darkness, but I had used these stairs enough to be familiar with them. I moved slowly, feeling my way along the wall. The steps were narrow, treacherous, and they were damp now. Rain came in through cracks in the wall, and it pounded with such force I felt sure the bricks would cave in. I heaved a sigh of relief as my feet touched the base-ment floor.

I felt along the wall for the light switch. It was per-haps foolish to risk turning on the light, but one could carry caution just so far. The chances were few that anyone would see it at this hour of the night, and even I was not brave enough to walk down that base-ment hall in pitch-black darkness. I found the switch. The light blazed for a moment, then settled to a murky yellow glow. The cats were restless in their room. I could hear them stirring around, purring loudly. They scratched on the door, no doubt aware of my presence and already disturbed by the storm. I hurried toward the wooden staircase that led upstairs. My footsteps sounded like staccato explosions on the concrete floor. I stooped down to remove my shoes.

I moved up the wooden staircase. Each step had its own individual squeak, a piercing wooden shriek, a dull groan. There was no banister, just as there was none on the tower stairs, and I had to lean against the wall for support. I walked quickly down the narrow little hall, my stockinged feet making no noise at all. I turned the corner and started to go down the side corridor. I stopped dead still. I had forgotten about the broken windowpanes.

One side of the corridor was solid with heavy oak paneling, but the other was entirely composed of curtainless windows that looked out over the gardens. The rain pounded against the glass with incredible velocity, as though it would smash and shatter. Several of the panes were already broken, I remembered, and the rain splashing through them now reminded me sharply of that fact. Pools of water stood along the floor, and it was as though someone had turned on an indoor sprinkling system. It would be impossible to pass down the corridor without getting soaking wet. Violent flashes of lightning illuminated the scene and pointed out the folly of such a course.

I hesitated for several minutes. I contemplated going back the way I had come, using the other door in my room and going downstairs by way of the main staircase. It would take too much time. Honora was waiting for me. She probably wondered what on earth had happened to me. I took a deep breath and ran down the corridor, moving haphazardly and entirely without grace. I slid in a puddle of water and almost fell down. A sudden gust of rain struck me directly in the face. I dropped one of my shoes and had to waste seconds retrieving it. When I reached the end of the corridor I looked as though I had been tossed into the briny sea and pulled out just short of drowning.

I shivered and wiped damp tendrils of hair away from my temples. I wanted to cry like a child, but I had brought all this on myself by being so careless, and doubtless deserved every bit of it. If I caught cold, it would serve me right, I told myself, and even as I scolded I knew that it was a form of whistling in the dark. I was scared spitless and had just enough sense left to keep from giving in to it. I shook my skirt, smoothed my hair back. I tried to remember the way Andrea and I had come that morning when she had first shown me the tower room. Did I turn to my left or to my right?

I walked down a dark hall. A lamp was burning in a room ahead, and it gave just enough illumination for me to find my way without going into a wall. I pushed open a door and stepped into a small study. It had the smell of man—leather, tobacco, sweat—and there was a desk cluttered with papers. I passed through it and into a small hallway that I knew would bring me out just below the staircase.

A lamp was burning in the main hall, near the front door, but there were no signs that anyone was up. Within, the house was still, while outside the storm raged furiously. That beating and pounding only intensified the solemn quiet that reigned here. I peered around the corner. A large potted plant blocked my line of vision. This part of the hall was a nest of shad-

ows, and there was a curious noise that I hadn't noticed before. Then I realized that it was the ticking of
the ornate clock that stood directly across from me.

It was after twelve-thirty. Honora must have given
me up. I must get the purse and get back up to her
quickly. In the state of mind she was in, there was no
telling what she might do if she thought I wasn't going to come. I crept behind the plant and looked
around the waxy green leaves. There was no one in
sight, but I had the strange impression that someone
had just been here. The air seemed to retain the im-
pressions made by recent movement through it. A
clap of thunder exploded, and the front windows rattled as though someone were trying to break in.

I seemed to be paralyzed. I had to force myself to
move.

My heart was pounding rapidly as I edged along the
wall to the door of the drawing room. If someone
came and saw me, I would have quite an explanation
to make. That I had come after my purse sounded
reasonable enough; that I had slipped stealthily
around the back way and gotten myself drenched in
the process looked highly suspicious. I slipped into
the drawing room. There was just enough light coming through the open door for me to see the outlines
of the furniture. I moved quickly to the table where I
had left my purse. It was still there. It did not seem to
have been touched. I picked it up and gave a deep
sigh of relief. Now I could go on up to Honora's
room.

I was leaving the drawing room and had almost
stepped out into the hall when I heard the noise. For a
moment it seemed my heart had stopped beating. I
stepped back into the shadows of the room. My throat

was dry, and my knees seemed suddenly unable to support the weight of my body. I clutched the arm of a chair, listening.

The noise was repeated. A board creaked. It came from the staircase. The noises of the storm were muted, and this new sound rang out sharply in the stillness of the hall. Someone was on the stairs. I could not tell if they were going up or coming down, but they were moving as slowly and stealthily as I had a few moments before. Time seemed to hang suspended. I waited, holding my breath, knowing that any moment now I might let out a scream that would be heard on the outskirts of London. The noise was not repeated. I decided that it had all been my imagination. I stepped boldly into the hall and looked at the staircase. Velvety black shadows poured down the steps, but there was no one there.

I bent down to put my shoes on. I felt slightly ashamed of myself. I needed to be resolute and firm of purpose, and here I was acting like a young idiot. I should have marched brazenly downstairs, leaving a trail of lights blazing behind me, and if I had run into anyone, I should have boldly told them I had forgotten my purse. Now, wet, bedraggled, trembling, I couldn't face anyone.

I had no intentions of going back the way I had come. Once through that indoor shower system was enough. I remembered that I had left the light burning in the basement. Let it burn, I thought. The waste of electricity wouldn't wreck the economic foundations and leave the family bankrupt. When Andrea discovered it burning in the morning, she'd think one of the servants had turned it on. The ornate clock ticked loudly. It was three minutes till one. I had been down here for almost twenty minutes. I must delay no longer.

I started up the staircase. The best way to conquer fear is to meet it head on, I told myself, and although my whole body seemed to quiver, my step did not falter as I moved slowly up through that cascade of shadows. When I reached the top, something touched my shoulder. I closed my eyes and waited for the end, only to feel the smooth texture of a leaf stroking my cheek.

I stood at the head of the stairs for a moment, trying to think of some sort of plan. I knew what Honora was going to tell me. In my heart I knew. Once those words were spoken, I couldn't stay at Blackcrest, nor could she. We would leave, storm or no storm. We would go to Alex, and we would wait there until Martin Craig came. Then Honora could tell the detective what she knew, and it would all be over. Honora's word was all we needed. With the things I had uncovered this afternoon, it would be enough. If only she would tell me. If only she hadn't lost her nerve and decided to keep her secret. . . . I hurried down the hall. The girl must be terrified now, knowing what she knew, waiting to unmask the man who had sent her lover away.

The draperies were parted on the windows at the end of the hall, and flashes of lightning illuminated that area, silver-blue explosions that shattered the darkness and tossed darting black shadows over the walls. I moved toward that light, confident now, not at all afraid, or so I told myself. I was directly in front of the windows now. I could glimpse storm-tossed limbs outside. The rain did not seem to be falling so furiously now. There had been no thunder for some time. The storm was abating, the wind and lightning throwing their last furious volleys before dying down completely.

I made a turn and walked down a short, narrow hallway that connected with the one in back that would eventually lead me to the top of the servants' stairs and the passageway to the tower-room door. I had decided to dry off and change before going to Honora. It would take only a few minutes more, and I would be much better prepared to face her if I looked at least halfway human.

I moved down the back hall. It made curious twists and turns, but I knew my way around well enough to be sure that I was going in the right direction. I was halfway down the hall when a tremendous clap of thunder exploded. The walls around me seemed to tremble. There was a moment of sheer pandemonium followed by something like a gigantic shudder, and then the storm was over, abruptly. The sudden stillness following that great upheaval was completely unnerving. Blackcrest seemed to pause, suspended in space, and then the walls around me became familiar, sinister. No longer tormented by the storm, they watched me, waiting for an opportunity to close in, smother.

I could hear my own breathing. It sounded frightfully loud, and the echoes of the soft sound reverberated about me as though the walls, too, were breathing with short, gasping breaths. I shivered. The air was icy cold, and it stirred in a chilly current, as though a door or window had been left open somewhere nearby. The normal noises of the house resumed: a window rattled against its frame, a floorboard creaked, the house settled back into its mold like a body stretched tight and suddenly relaxing the tension. I started to walk on down the hall, determined to banish all this fanciful thought and concentrate on the job that waited for me.

I could see the opening in the wall ahead where the servants' staircase came up. There was a window over the landing, and just enough misty gray light came through to sharpen the black outlines of the banister post and railing. I moved toward it, knowing that I would soon be in my room. I was heedless of noise now. My heels tapped on the floor, and I walked quickly. I was perhaps twenty yards from the staircase when that darker shadow moved, wavered, disappeared into the opening, and merged with the others. It happened so quickly I couldn't be sure I had seen anything at all.

The window over the landing rattled violently as a sudden gust of wind struck it. The noise was not alarming, but it was loud enough to cover any other noise—footsteps moving hastily down the stairs. I hesitated for only a second. I rushed toward the staircase. I leaned over the railing and peered down into that vault of blackness. There was no disturbance there. The curtain over the window flapped out, causing a dark shadow to flicker across the gray wall. No doubt that was what I had seen.

I went toward the tower room. I passed Honora's door. A thin line of light showed under the bottom of her door. She was still up, still waiting for me. I had an impulse to knock on the door and go right in, but since I had taken this long, a few minutes more wouldn't matter. As I walked down the hall, I smelled a sharp, curious odor. It was strong and pungent, like turpentine or ammonia. I wondered if one of the servants had knocked over a can of cleaning fluid recently.

My room seemed beautifully familiar after the dark halls, a bright nest that had my own personal touch. Various clothes were strewn about, vivid splotches of color against the subdued glow of the lamp. Now that I was warm and safe, the other seemed a nightmare. I tossed the bag on the bed. It landed with a thump, and the catch snapped open. The gun slid out, a hideous black thing that made me shudder. It gleamed in the soft light. I stuck it hastily back in the bag, jerked open the top drawer of the nightstand, and dumped the bag inside.

I did not want to go to Honora's room. I knew I must, but I knew what I must hear, and I didn't want to hear it. I took off the wet dress and draped it over the open door of the wardrobe. I slowly peeled off the soaked stockings and put them aside. I didn't want to go. I wanted to delay it as long as possible, and I knew in my heart that going down after the purse had been merely another delaying tactic, however subconscious it might have been at the time. I could easily have gone for the purse first thing in the morning, before the others were up. Honora was going to tell me something, and I didn't know if I had the ability to hear it without complete collapse.

For a few moments more I wanted to cling to hope, to that foolish certainty that Delia was alive and well. Missing—but alive and well. I knew Honora would shatter that illusion.

I took out a fresh dress, dark topaz cotton, and put it on. I took up the brush again and brushed some life back into the damp russet waves. My face was still pale, the skin stretched tightly over the high cheekbones, and my eyes looked more green than blue. They stared back at me, afraid. Going to hear Honora's secret would take far more courage than it had taken to go downstairs in the dark. Now that the moment had come when I must go, I felt weak. I wanted to run. I wanted to hide. I did not want to hear the full details of what she had merely hinted at this evening at the foot of the stairs.

I braced myself.

"This is it, duckie," I said, imitating Tottie. I wondered why I should think of her at a moment like this.

I opened the door to the hall, grimly determined to face the truth now and be done with it. The odor of cleaning fluid assailed my nostrils immediately. It seemed even stronger now, and I coughed. Betty must have been in the hall, polishing the wainscoting. I wondered why I hadn't smelled it earlier when I was going down for dinner. I went to the door of Honora's room and knocked quietly. My eyes were smarting. Honora did not answer. I called her name and knocked again. The door swung open. I stepped into the room.

It was a beautiful room. The walls were papered with ivory embossed with tiny blue fleurs-de-lis. The carpet was dark blue, thick; the furniture white, the satiny surface of the wood gleaming. There was a blue-and-lilac canopy over the bed. The bed was made up, the lilac counterpane smooth and unrumpled. The odor of cleaning fluid was so strong that I almost fainted. My head whirled. My eyes were blinded by sharp, smarting tears.

I stumbled across the room to the window. I tried to force it open. It was locked. There was no time to fumble with the clasp. Already I could feel myself growing numb, black wings pressing my brain. I wadded the material of my skirt around my fist and smashed the window. It broke with a great crash. Sharp, jagged pieces of glass fell at my feet. Cold air rushed into the room. I gasped. I leaned on the windowsill and took great gulps of air.

There were two more windows in the room. I broke both of them. The cold air soared into the room, swirling away those deadly fumes that had hung like a pall from floor to ceiling, destroying me. I was steady now. My eyes still smarted, but the dizziness had gone. Honora was not in the room. I saw the door to the bathroom. It was closed.

I opened it.

She was on the floor. She wore a sky-blue nightgown with lace ruffles at the throat and wrists, the sort of nightgown a little girl might wear. Her lips were slightly parted, and her eyes were closed as though she were sleeping. The can of cleaning fluid was turned over beside her, the murderous liquid all evaporated into the air. Draped over the bathtub was the yellow dress she had worn to dinner. She had removed only a few of the red stains before the fumes had overcome her.

17

It was called carbon tetrachloride. The caution on the side of the can plainly stated that it should be used only outdoors, or if applied inside, with windows opened and fresh air circulating. Honora had not read the warning. She had taken the can into the small bathroom with its one window tightly closed, shut the door behind her, and accidentally knocked the can over. The doctor said that the fumes must have overcome her before she could get to the window. It was a sad, sad accident, he said as he signed the death certificate.

I was not sure it was an accident.

Last night, when they had come bursting into the room after hearing the windows crash, I had been in a state of shock. When Derek Hawke came toward me in his blue pajamas and black robe, I had been unable to say anything. I pointed to the bathroom floor, my eyes full of tears. Then I fainted. He carried me to my room. Later, much later, the doctor gave me a sedative, and now I had made my statement, the policeman and the doctor had gone, and a hearse had taken the body away. The house had that terrible silence that always follows death.

Andrea was in her room, under sedation, and the servants went about their tasks on tiptoes, speaking in whispers when it was necessary to speak at all. Derek Hawke had been on the phone all morning long, talking in a low voice to persons unknown. I knew that at least two of the calls had been long distance. Honora was gone, and already he was making legal arrangements to see that her considerable fortune was disposed of to his satisfaction. It would all go to Andrea, of course, and therefore to him.

It was almost three o'clock now. I was in the drawing room. Betty had brought me a luncheon tray, insisting that I eat something, but the tray rested on the coffee table, the food untouched. The draperies were open, and dazzling sunlight danced into the room in wavering rays. The day was beautiful, the sky a vivid blue, the air fresh and pure. Rain had washed the earth clean, and the trees displayed gorgeous greenery that shimmered in the gentle breeze. Everything should have been gray and bleak. Nature seemed to mock tragedy.

I had tried to call Alex around noon, but I could not reach him. I had tried a second time a short while ago, but he still had not answered his phone. I had to talk to him. I had to tell him what I had seen last night. I was certain now that the figure at the top of the back staircase had not been my imagination. Martin Craig was supposed to come to Hawkestown today. Alex was probably with the detective, and they were probably verifying the things I had told Alex yesterday. He had said he would call. I did not think I could sit still in this house and wait any longer. I had to do something.

Betty came into the drawing room. Her eyes were red-rimmed, her face lined with grief, but she was curiously calm and serene. She had spent part of the morning at the chapel, and there was a noble resignation about her that only a strong faith can bring. She gently admonished me for not eating. I told her it was impossible. She stepped over to a table and began to polish the surface with the edge of her apron. I saw that she didn't want to leave just yet. She wanted to talk.

"I left that can upstairs myself," she said quietly. "There was a terrible spot on one of the carpets, and I needed somethin' strong. I put the can in my broom closet. If I'd taken it back down, she wouldn't of used it. It's my fault."

"No, Betty," I said. "Don't talk like that."

"My poor love, my angel. She didn't know nothin' about them cleanin' things. She must of thought it was just regular spot remover like I used on her clothes sometimes."

"Don't," I said. "Please don't."

"I'm sorry, Miss Deborah. I know how you must feel—findin' her an' all. I just don't know what's goin' to happen now. Without my angel here this house won't be the same. I won't be able to stay. I'll have to leave, like Jake."

"Where did he go?" I asked. "Do you know?"

"He has a brother in Devon who owns a nursery. Raises shrubs, rose bushes, an' things. He's wanted Jake to join him for a long time, was always writin' and askin' him to come. Jake's already left Hawkestown. He must be on his way to Devon right now. I'll write to him. He'll want to know. He worshiped Miss Honora, just like all the rest of us. I remember when she was a little girl an' had her own garden, an' he would help her with the flowers."

"What about Neil?" I asked before she could continue with her reverie. "Is he with his father?"

Betty shook her head. She finished polishing the table and looked around for something else to do. She went over to the mantel and began to rearrange the Dresden figurines that sat on it.

"Does he know?" I asked.

"I told him this morning. I stopped to see him after I came out of the chapel. He's stayin' with a friend of his who lives at a boardinghouse in town. He was stunned. He couldn't say anything. I patted him on the shoulder an' left. He needed to be alone."

"He must have taken it hard," I said.

"He loved her, Miss Deborah. He was a wild one in ways, an' I was worried about Miss Honora at first, but he loved her. I know he did. I saw the way he was with her—protective an' all. He wanted to wait till she was of age, but it was her who was so anxious. She wanted to get away from *him*. He hated Neil. Just because the boy had all that hair an' drove a motor-scooter an' worked at that place—" She paused, shaking her head. "Even if he did get in trouble once or twice, even if he did steal those radios from the hardware store, that didn't mean he was all bad. She was reformin' him. He stopped all that when they got serious."

"I know, Betty," I replied.

"They was still plannin' to run off together. Miss Honora ran after him yesterday after *he* threw the boy out. I heard 'em talkin' on the back steps. I was in the kitchen, an' I heard 'em makin' plans. She intended to meet him today. He wanted 'er to come with 'im right then, but she said she had to stay. She said she had to get back at *him*. She said she had something to tell—I don't know what. Neil told her she'd better forget about it an' not stir up trouble. He said there'd be trouble enough when they ran off."

"I want to talk to him," I said. "Tell me how to get to the boardinghouse."

Betty gave me directions. I stood up, eager to be gone. There was something to do at last. I was wearing a brown-and-green plaid skirt and a dark green sweater, but I wouldn't take the time to change into something more appropriate. Neil would be stunned with grief. He wouldn't notice what I was wearing. Betty sensed my tension. She seemed to be a bit apprehensive about my going.

"Are you sure you ought to be drivin'?" she asked. "You're still in a state, an' that drug the doctor gave you—"

"I'm perfectly all right, Betty. Don't . . . don't tell anyone where I have gone. Will you promise not to?"

"Of course, Miss Deborah, but—"

"If anyone asks, just say you don't know. I must hurry. . . ."

I seemed to be in a trance. I drove mechanically, automatically doing all the things required of me but conscious of none of them. I saw none of the scenery, and the road was merely a gray-brown ribbon unfolding beneath the wheels. My mind was occupied with other things, and the driving might have been done by another Deborah Lane who was miraculously able to avoid an accident while I was thinking about Neil.

He would help me. I knew he would. After what Derek Hawke had done, he would be ready to stand up to him and see that justice was done. Betty had told me that Neil had warned Honora to "forget about it and not stir up trouble." He knew. Honora must have told him. She had been in the cellars, waiting to meet Neil, and she had seen something. It was only natural that she tell Neil. He would help me now. He must. If only I could gain his confidence. If only he weren't so grief-stricken that he wouldn't be able to realize the importance of it all.

I dreaded going to him. I dreaded seeing his grief. For all his surly mannerisms and his rebellious facade, I knew that there was a deep sensitivity in his makeup. Otherwise Honora would not have loved him. He was very young, and the very young feel things so strongly. He would be bereft, and I would have to bring up painful things that wouldn't make his loss any easier to bear. It was not going to be pleasant.

I arrived at the edge of Hawkestown with a sense of shock. I hadn't paid the least attention to the road, and here I was already. I looked for the turnoff Betty had mentioned and drove a short way down a street lined with old frame houses with peeling paint and sagging roofs. The place I was looking for was at the end of the block, a three-story brown frame house with gables and an overabundance of gingerbread trim around the wooden veranda. I saw the motorcycle parked at one side of the house under a decrepit oak tree. Three dirty children in tattered clothes were examining the machine with wondrous eyes.

The woman who answered my knock had a face that looked as though it had long since lost the ability to express emotion of any kind. Her hennaed hair was wet and in steel curlers, and a shabby red chenille robe covered her plump middle-aged body. A cigarette dangled from her lips. She did not remove it when she spoke. I asked for Neil. She jerked her head toward the stairs and said he was in the second room on the left. She stood with her hands on her hips, watching me as I started up. Her black eyes were as void of life as a zombie's. The stairs were dark and creaked alarmingly as I went up them. The whole house reeked with the odor of recently cooked cabbage.

I heard the music as soon as I reached the second floor. It was one of the earliest Beatles records, and it blared brazenly. I wondered if whoever was playing it knew of the grief in the house. I stepped to the door of the room the woman had indicated, and I was rather perturbed to find that the music was coming from that room. I knocked loudly, hoping Neil could hear the knock over that blaring music. Music soothes, but I doubted if that particular kind of music could be said to qualify under these circumstances. There was a screeching whir as the needle was raked across the surface of the record, then blessed silence. I could hear his footsteps as he walked toward the door.

"What do you want?" he said sullenly, staring at me with dark eyes that didn't try to hide their dislike.

"I've come about Honora," I told him.

"I've already heard about it. The maid told me this morning."

"I . . . I would like to talk to you," I said gently.

He hesitated for just a moment. Then he held the door open. "Be my guest," he said in that same sullen voice.

I stepped into the room. It was dirty and disorderly. Pop posters were tacked all over one wall, and a pile of records leaned against the cheap portable phonograph that sat on the floor beside the unmade bed. I could smell sweat and grease and the odor of soiled clothing. Neil stood just inside the room, a defiant grin on his lips as he watched my reactions to the mess.

"I wasn't expecting company," he said.

"That's quite apparent," I replied coldly.

"Place belongs to a friend of mine. He's a slob."

I must be fair to him, I told myself. It was only natural that he be rude and sullen. I came from Blackcrest, and Blackcrest was enemy territory. He might even think that Derek Hawke had sent me to deliver some message or make some threat. Naturally he would be uneasy and on guard. Nevertheless, I could feel his animosity, and I didn't like the way his dark eyes leered at me. Be fair, I warned myself as my defenses rose, be fair.

"Make yourself at home," he said. "I'm busy."

He stepped over to a chipped dresser and began to take clothes out of the top drawer. He chose to ignore me while he did this. I wondered how I was going to overcome his animosity. I wondered how I was going to penetrate that barrier. He wore black boots, skin-tight gray pants, and a silky gray shirt with enormous blue and purple flowers. The shirt hung loose over the pants, and the sleeves were full-gathered at the wrists. With his shaggy blond hair and full sneering lips, he looked like a virile young animal, uncouth and dangerous. I told myself that this was the boy Honora loved, a boy who was too proud to show his grief to a stranger.

"I . . . I know how you must feel," I said. "I wish there were something I could say—"

"Spare me," he snarled.

"Neil—I'm on your side."

"Really?" He stopped what he was doing and looked at me, one brow arched arrogantly.

"I understand. Honora . . . spoke of you. She told me how she felt. I thought she was very lucky to be so young and . . . so in love."

"Yeah?"

"Yes," I said calmly. "She told me about the . . . opposition. I know how hard it must have been."

"It's over now," he said bluntly. "Water under the dam."

"You don't know what Derek Hawke has done," I protested.

"I don't particularly care."

"If you knew—"

"Baby," he said, "I'm busy. Get to the point."

I cringed at the "baby." I stared at him with frosty eyes.

"Very well. Honora told me she saw something down in the cellars, about six weeks ago. She was about to tell me about it, but we were interrupted. I . . . I need to know what she saw. It's imperative that I know. She said she was waiting for you at the time. She must have told you about it."

"That?" he said, scowling. "She babbled about it for weeks. She was always seeing things, imagining things. She was nervous, jumpy. She said she saw Hawke going down in the cellars with a woman. She was hiding behind one of the wine racks. She said they were laughing and carrying on as they disappeared into one of the rooms. She heard a scream. When Hawke came out, the woman wasn't with him."

So I knew now. It was a fact. There could be no more hope. I took it with amazing calm. The boy stood with his hands on his thighs, looking at me with a sarcastic smile.

"She was lying," he said.

"How do you know?"

"He's cool," Neil said, "real cool. He might commit murder, but he wouldn't be careless enough to do it in his own cellars."

"Then why did Honora tell you that?"

He frowned, his lips curling in disgust. "She wanted attention. I didn't show that night. There was a poker game afterward when we closed up the joint. She was waiting for me, and I didn't show. She was still waiting when I came in—all hysterical. I told her to cool it. She was like that, always playing for attention, always wanting to know everything I did. It chapped."

"Honora was telling the truth," I said flatly.

He paused. He shook his head slowly. "Wow," he said, stretching the word out.

"It's true. The . . . the woman was my cousin. Hawke murdered her. I found her scarf in the cellars. I . . . I've gathered evidence against him. A detective is working on the case."

"No kiddin'," he said.

"Will you help me?" I asked. "Will you repeat what you've just told me to the detective? Will you sign a statement?"

He grunted. "Un-unh. Not this baby."

"Of course you will," I said.

"Look—I'm not getting involved," he said slowly. "No cops, no statements. No commitments. Not this baby. Not me."

"You can't mean that," I said, stunned.

"I mean every word of it, baby. I'm leaving for London tonight. I don't intend to get messed up with this. You play girl detective all you want, but leave me out of it."

"Neil! Derek Hawke committed murder! He . . . he may have murdered Honora—"

"Tough," he said. His voice was flat, unmoved.

I stood there, unable to comprehend it. Neil took out a suitcase and began to toss clothes into it. He was calm, completely unperturbed by what I had just told him. The hideous silk shirt swung to and fro as he moved. The boots scraped on the bare wooden floor. He wiped a strand of hair away from his temple and continued to pack. I couldn't believe it. For a moment I simply couldn't believe it.

"But—you loved her—" I protested.

"Come off it," he snapped. "Sure, I played around. For a while I thought there might be something in it. She wanted to elope. I knew he would have my hide— there was some trouble earlier with the cops, and he would bring that up. Why not? I thought. She was eager. I figured I had a good thing going. If I could hold her off till she was eighteen, I stood to make quite a haul. Wishful thinking. Hawke wasn't about to let anything like that happen. Shame," he said, shaking his head, "but I'll latch onto something good in London. There's lots of lonely birds there with lots of money."

"He was right," I whispered. "Derek Hawke was right about you."

"You thought it was the big romance?"

"I suppose I did," I replied, my voice like ice.

He chuckled. "So did she. Women are fools."

"Yes," I said, "we are."

"I played the big scene yesterday after he canned the old man. Didn't have nothing to lose, thought he might even give me some money if I said I'd keep away from her. No dice, and I mean but *no* dice. He threw me out."

"And you still let her think you were going to elope with her," I said.

"Sure, Honora ran after me. I knew it was a losing proposition. I let her babble on. I listened to her silly plans. I was planning to move out, and I didn't want no hysterical farewell scene. So I let her talk. I played the game."

"And Honora lost."

"Looks that way, baby."

"No," I said quietly. "No one can be that cold, that callous. She is dead, *dead*! You must have some feeling."

"It don't pay, baby. This is the twentieth century. Romeo and Juliet are way, way out of style."

I slapped him then. I drew back my palm and smashed it against his face. It landed with a sharp impact. He cried out in shock. He stared at me with a stunned expression, and for a moment I thought he was going to seize me. I stood my ground, glaring at him with a hard, cold anger that blazed through my body. With my eyes I dared him to say or do anything. He rubbed his cheek. He nodded at me as though we were playing a game and I had scored that

round. I turned and left the room, trembling with
rage. I was still trembling when I got in the car.

I drove around for a long time, the anger possess-
ing me with hard, merciless force. Thirty minutes
passed, and I found myself by the edge of the river,
staring at the water and the drooping willow trees.
That first fury was dissipated now. It left by degrees,
and I found my mind working with cold, mechanical
precision. I knew what I was going to do. I couldn't
wait for Alex. I couldn't wait for Martin Craig. I drove
to a drugstore and purchased a flashlight. I stepped
into the phone booth and dialed Alex's number. The
phone rang several times. I tapped my fingernails impatiently on the instrument panel.

A woman answered. For a moment I didn't recognize her voice.

"Mr. Tanner," I said.

"He's out. This is . . . his secretary."

"Deborah Lane speaking," I replied crisply. "This is
very important. Tell him I *know for sure*. He'll understand. Tell him I've gone down to the cellars to find
the . . . the place."

"But, duckie—"

"Tell him to hurry," I said.

I hung up the phone. I got into the car and drove
back to Blackcrest. The gun was in the purse at my
side. The flashlight was strong, its battery new. I had
had enough evasion, enough of piecing together a
horrible jigsaw puzzle. Now I intended to act.

18

I closed the cellar door behind me. It was not likely that anyone would come down and see it open, but I wouldn't take that chance. I shut it firmly and switched on the flashlight. The strong light swept over the area like a silver-white blade, pointing out the damp, dangerous steps and the rough brown wall with its festoons of wet green fungus. I went down the steps cautiously. I was incredibly calm, incredibly firm of purpose. Now that I knew, nothing remained but to locate the final, irrefutable evidence and be done with it. I suppose I was in shock. Grief and horror would come later, but now I moved as though in a trance.

I had the gun with me. I held it at my side, my fingers curled around the cold black metal. It was a heavy, awkward thing, and I was tempted to hide it at the foot of the steps. I did not know if I could pull the trigger if the need arose. I doubted it. For a moment I hesitated, thinking I would slip it behind the bottom

step. Then I decided against it. The gun seemed un-
necessarily dramatic, but there was a certain security
in having it with me. I kept it in my hand.

I moved past the wine racks. I passed through the
first room, trying to remember the way I had gone
yesterday morning when I was pursuing the kitten. I
turned down a narrow passage that brought me into a
small room with rusty tools leaning against the walls.
There was a shovel and a pick. The shovel had dried
mud caked on it. The room was a dead end. I retraced
my way and went down a second passage. It took me
into the room with the kegs.

The silence of the place was unnerving. It was broken only by the faint drip of water that seeped down
a wall from some invisible source. Motes of dust
danced in the beam of my flashlight, and a broken
cobweb swayed from the ceiling in a rhythmic motion, to and fro in the gentle current of air caused by
my movement. I saw the table where the kitten had
perched in such terror. I moved toward the passage I
had followed yesterday.

I stumbled on a piece of wood. It clattered under
my foot, and the echoes of the noise shattered the
silence. The noise reverberated in the air for a moment and then died down. The silence that followed
was even more intense by contrast. It seemed to be
laden with inaudible noises, those same silent whispers I had sensed yesterday morning. The fumes of
alcohol were overwhelming. There was, too, a sour
odor, sharp and unpleasant. I switched the blade of
light around the room. It glided over huge wooden
kegs, washed the dank walls.

I started down the passage. I might have been in the
bowels of the earth. The great weight of Blackcrest

was above me, and the celing of the passage seemed to sag down, inch by inch. I could visualize a complete collapse of the foundations. I could see tons of earth and rubble falling with one sudden thud, crushing me, or worse, leaving me trapped here, buried alive. The thought was horrible. Threats of claustrophobia swept over me, and my body tightened. I gnawed my lower lip, standing still for a moment, banishing the morbid fear.

I moved on, trying not to think. This was no time for thinking. I couldn't allow my mind to swerve from its grim purpose. If I did, if I loosened one bit, lost one fraction of control, I knew I would crumble into a hysterical mass, capable of nothing but piercing screams. In a short while it would all be over. I would find what I was looking for. Alex would come. Derek Hawke would be unmasked. I would go away for a while. I would be completely alone. I would grieve, and I would come to grips with the horror of it all. Now I must not waver.

The passage made a sloping turn, widened. I was in the main passage now. The beam of my light picked out the ancient wooden doors ahead. I remembered the rusty chains I had seen on the wall of one of those cells and shuddered at the thought of them. The heels of my shoes scraped the earthen floor. The sound was magnified in the stillness. This part of the cellars was icy cold. Zephyrs of clammy air stroked my cheeks. I wondered where the air could possibly be coming from.

I was almost in that great cavern of a room at the end of the passage, the place where I had found the scarf. I passed by the doors of the cells. I stopped. I stood dead still for a moment. My heart seemed to leap in my breast; then it pattered rapidly. Every fiber of my body was taut, concentrating. I heard a noise, far behind me, coming from that section of the cellars I had already passed through. Footsteps? I could not be sure.

The noise had been there for some time, but I had been so engrossed in thought that it had not fully registered. Now it had brought me up sharp, banishing everything else. Footsteps? Had I heard footsteps? I hardly dared breathe. I stood rigid, my eyes closed.

I listened. There were no footsteps. I was nervous and on edge. I had imagined them. There was another sound. It was almost like heavy breathing, as though someone else, behind me, had paused to listen. I trembled. The cold air stroked my face and arms. How foolish. I heaved a sigh of relief. The acoustics of the place magnified each tiny noise; the echoes repeated it over and over. The air swirled around the walls, and it sounded like breathing. I gripped the flashlight and started to move on.

The sudden clatter exploded in the silence. Someone had stumbled on a piece of wood, possibly the same one I had stumbled on. It was not my overactive imagination this time. The noise was real, the echoes still ricocheting it from wall to wall. The door of the last cell was open. I darted into the cell. The beam of my light flashed on the wall, showing me the chains that hung there. I switched the light off.

I don't know how long I stayed there in the cell. Time seemed to have no meaning. There was just the darkness, and me, and that presence out there. The last echo had vanished. I listened for other sounds in the darkness, but my heart was pounding so loudly that I could not be sure that I heard anything else. I could not hear, but I could feel. I could feel that other presence, feel its evil. The evil was all around me. It seemed to come closer and closer, waiting to claim me, waiting to destroy me. My fear was a tangible thing.

Time passed. Nothing happened. There were no new noises. My body grew stiff from standing in one position for so long. Tiny pinpricks of pain jabbed my legs, and I knew they would soon be cramped if I did not move them. It was cold, terribly cold, and the clammy air swirled into the cell in icy currents. I had not noticed this coldness yesterday morning. There had certainly been no currents then, only the horrible stillness.

I had turned the flashlight off, but gradually my eyes had become accustomed to the dreadful darkness in the cell. It was no larger than eight feet square, and the ceiling was not six feet from the floor. The top of my head almost touched it. After a while I could see the outlines of the chains, dark black against the grayish black of the wall. Manacles dangled from the end of them, and I wondered what wrists had been fastened in those terrible iron bands, what person or persons had been confined in this cell, staring at the walls in darkness and surely feeling no more terror than I felt at this moment.

Centuries had passed since this cell was built. Customs had changed radically, but man had not changed at all. One of Derek Hawke's ancestors had ruled here, a blackhearted tyrant who could confine his victims in a cell, leave them to die while he carried on with his treachery, and Hawke was no different. The twentieth century had given him a civilized facade. He could not be so open in his treachery, so

flamboyant in his vices, but he was no different from
that earlier Hawke. These thoughts raced through my
mind as I waited, listening, trembling.

I stood up straight. I rubbed my arms. The gun in
my hand seemed an afterthought, a foolish piece of
excess baggage that was of no use at all. I had forgotten I even had it, the fingers that gripped it numb
now. Fifteen minutes had passed, perhaps thirty. No
one had come down the passage. No footsteps had
echoed along the walls. I switched on the flashlight.
The beam landed directly on the grave in the corner
of the cell.

There was no question about it. It was a grave. The
mound of earth on top was loose, that around it
tightly packed. I remembered the shovel I had seen
earlier, its blade caked with dried mud. I stared at the
mound of earth. I had been inches away from it as I
leaned against the wall. It had been at my feet.

I felt none of the things I thought I should feel. I
should scream, I told myself. I should faint. I was
emotionless. I stared at the grave, and I thought: It is
over. My part is done. I can go now. Later I can
grieve.

I stepped out of the cell. I stepped directly into his
arms. I did not see his face. I tried to cry out, but no
sound came. I dropped the flashlight. It shattered. We
were in darkness. His arms were holding me to him.

He released me. He struck a match. In its glow I
could see the wide mouth, the twisted nose, the dark
eyes, and the brows with their arrogant slant. He held
the match over the wick of an old oil lamp. I wondered where he had found the lamp. The wick caught,
glowed. The light spread slowly. He shielded the
flame for a moment and then set the lamp on the

floor. That flickering glow cast shadows all around us. They danced on the walls. His face was in shadow. I could see only the dark eyes.

"Deborah," he said.

"My God! Alex. I thought you were Derek Hawke." They were so alike. The features were so similar.

"Did you?" He laughed quietly.

"You frightened me. I thought—"

"Did I, now?" he said.

I knew then. I sensed it. He had said nothing more, but I knew. I could feel it. Always before there had been a gentle rush of warmth the moment I heard his voice, the moment I looked into those laughing eyes. It was not there now. Now there was an instinctive fear, and it was so strong that I backed away. The dark eyes looked at me. There was no laughter in them now. I backed against the wall and stood there, looking at his face, so shadowed, so like Derek's.

"You," I said.

"Yes. I wondered when you would discover it."

"How? Why? What . . . what do you intend to do?"

"One question at a time, please," he said. His voice was casual, a light, mocking voice that I had once found so pleasant.

"Delia—" I whispered.

"I met her at a party in Soho. She was an ardent fan of mine, had read every single book. She was beautiful and bright and full of sparkle, surrounded by a crowd of admiring males, but when she discovered who I was, she left the crowd. She came to me. Her eyes were full of awe, and she babbled for thirty minutes about the books, asked me how I got my plots, all the typical questions. I knew then that she was the one I needed. I had everything figured out, down to the last detail. I needed a woman, an actress, someone I could trust to do the job and do it without flaw."

"What are you talking about? I don't understand."

"My dear Deborah, do concentrate. It's my very best plot, much too good to be used in one of the books. Intricate, complicated, a stroke of genius." His voice had a hard, arrogant quality I had never heard in it before. I did not know this man. I had never known Alex Tanner. "Perhaps I shall use it someday," he continued, "though not in one of those cheap thrillers. No, this is too good for that."

"Tell me," I said.

"I shall do you that honor, before—well, we both know what I must do."

I made no reply. He tilted his head to one side. His lips stretched into a smile, and that smile remained fixed as he spoke.

"When I met Delia, I had two problems. One of them was a woman, a cheap little barmaid I had inadvertently become involved with. She was a fascinating creature, vile, a guttersnipe, straight out of the pages of *Of Human Bondage*. She was determined to make me marry her. She gave me an ultimatum: marriage or a smashing lawsuit. I had—uh, how shall I put it?—aborted her. Myself. I knew the procedures. I couldn't let her carry out her threat, and I certainly had no intentions of marrying her. My first problem."

"And your second?"

"Derek. Self-righteous, smug, hypocritical. I'd always hated him, ever since we were children together. Derek was the good one. Derek was the one who was patted on the head and rewarded for his good conduct. I was punished. I was the black sheep. The situation never changed. I am still the black sheep, and Derek is Andy's heir. Blackcrest means something to me. I was never a part of it. I was always the outsider. I want it. After I inherit it, I may burn it down, but I want to walk through this house one time and know that it's mine, know that I'll never be an outsider again. Frightfully simple, psychologically, I know. Stems back to my childhood and all that. But I want it. I couldn't stand by and see Derek inherit it. My second problem."

"How did Delia come into it?" I asked. My voice was barely audible.

"Tottie was planning to come to Hawkestown. She had obtained a job at the Tea Shoppe through a friend of hers. She intended to use it as her base, as a constant warning to me of what she could do if I didn't come to heel, and come to heel fast. I stalled her off— for a while. During that time I courted your cousin."

"She told me she was seeing Derek Hawke."

"Brilliant," he said. "She followed instructions brilliantly. We talked for hours that first night at the party. I told her I was in the middle of a difficult book and was uncertain about the whole premise of the plot. She was absorbed, listening to me as I explained. Could a woman—my heroine—build a case against a man she'd never met. Could she pretend to be passionately in love with him, convince her roommate that she was going to leave to marry him, then disappear for a while so that the man would, ultimately, be accused of her murder when she failed to show up? Delia was certain it was possible. I said it wasn't. She said she could prove it."

"So she told me she was seeing Derek," I said.

"Yes."

"All the while she was seeing you."

"All the while," he repeated.

"She had no idea what she was doing," I said. "No idea—"

"She thought it was a great lark. She was 'contributing to literature.' It was quite a lot of fun for her. I've never met anyone who was quite so simple, quite so naïve—charmingly so, of course, but naïve. She was like putty in my hands."

"How did you talk her into quitting the show and leaving? She was a responsible person—for all her frivolity. She wouldn't just quit like that as part of a lark."

"She fell in love with me. I asked her to marry me. I told her I couldn't marry until I finished the book—artistic temperament—and I asked her to keep on helping me. She would 'live' the book while I wrote it. She was worried about you. She didn't want to upset you, but I convinced her that after you found out about it you'd understand. We would invite you to our wedding—the real wedding—and everything would end happily ever after for all concerned."

I remembered how elated Delia had been during those weeks when she was going with "Derek Hawke." She seemed to sparkle with new life, and she was unable to talk of anything but the fascinating man who had given her a whole new outlook. "Derek Hawke" was the only man on earth, the prince charming she had been waiting for all her life. "Derek" was Alex, of course, and Alex had used all his powerful charm on her, using it like a weapon to draw her to him. I could see how easily she would succumb to that charm, and I could see how the "deception" would appeal to that frothy, childish streak in her nature.

"So she came to Hawkestown," I said. "She sent the telegram. She went to see the vicar. . . ."

"Oh, yes. That was part of the 'research.' She gave me copious details about both encounters. I told her they would be perfect for the book. She was as delighted as a child. We were really building up a case against Derek, she said. I told her Derek was an eccentric cousin who was in on the scheme, letting me use his name. She wanted to meet him. Of course, I couldn't permit that."

"Of course not," I said.

"She did everything I told her to—perfectly."

"And you killed her."

"Correction. I killed Tottie."

"Tottie? But Tottie is alive. I met her—"

"Your cousin is a marvelous actress. Her talents are wasted in the music halls."

19

I could only stare at him, a wild elation sweeping over me as I realized what he had just said. I remembered the flippant, vivacious girl at the Tea Shoppe. I remembered her saucy mannerisms and the mischievous sparkle in her eyes. There had been an affinity between us at once, and I had warmed to her immediately. I remembered the cheap makeup and the junky jewelry, the dime-store perfume and the artificial black hair. Of course it had been Delia. I could see that now, so clearly. How delighted she must have been to be able to fool me with her blatant masquerade.

"Delia is alive—"

"Very much so. Full of life, if you'll pardon a bad pun. I left her an hour or so ago. She told me you called. She delivered your message."

"I didn't know. I spoke to her. I saw her. I didn't know—"

"She was quite amused by your visit to the Tea

Shoppe. She knew you were here, of course. She assured me that you'd come. It was only a matter of time. You'd come, and when you found no trace of her, you would accuse Derek Hawke of murder. It worked out exactly as planned. You did your part well, too, Deborah. Quite well."

"The grave—" I said.

"Tottie came to Hawkestown. I met her at the station. I wooed her. I said I had decided to marry her. I wanted to take her to see the family estate. I brought her here. I brought her down to the cellars. You know the rest."

"Honora saw you. She thought you were Derek."

"Correct."

"You killed her, too."

"At first—when you told me about what she'd seen —I thought I'd have to kill her, and then I realized she was my best witness. What she saw fit perfectly into my scheme. She saw *Derek* go down into the cellars with a woman, and of course I intended for Derek to be blamed for the murder of your cousin. Derek and I look very much alike. She thought *he* had taken the woman down here, and she was there to tell the world about it. I didn't kill Honora. It was what it appeared to be, an accident, a tragic accident."

"I don't believe you."

"Come, Deborah. Why should I lie—now?"

"I saw someone at the top of the servants' stairs last night."

"I doubt it. You must have imagined it."

He was right, of course. I had imagined it. I had been nervous and frightened, and the curtain had flapped out, throwing a shadow across the wall. I had imagined the footstep on the main staircase, too. It was an old house, full of strange noises, and the storm had not helped matters any. There had been nothing in the corridors last night besides me, and my fear.

"To continue," he said, "I murdered Tottie. She was a slut. She deserved everything she got. But—and this is that brilliant stroke of genius I mentioned—Tottie arrived in Hawkestown. Tottie took a job at the Tea Shoppe. Tottie is very much alive, but *Delia* had vanished. Everything is nicely in place."

"But Derek—"

"Derek will be accused of murder. Your murder. You've done exactly what I intended for you to do. You've asked questions, aroused suspicion. You've been searching for your missing cousin. When the police look for your body, they'll find not one, but two. Everyone will assume the other body is that of your cousin. You see, I planned it right down to the last detail, including your part."

"You intended to murder me? From the first?"

"From the very first."

"That night when you changed my tire—you knew?"

"Of course I did. That was a coincidence, meeting you like that." He laughed quietly. "I knew you'd come, but I was growing anxious. Six weeks had passed, and there had been no sign of you, and then I saw your car stranded on the road, and I knew immediately it was you. I was overjoyed. I could hardly contain my elation."

He stepped closer to me and lowered his voice.

"You were an essential part of the plan. The whole thing evolved around you. The woman I chose had to be gullible, but she also had to have a close friend o relative who would sound the alarm when she vanished. Delia talked about you that first night, about how close the two of you were."

He touched my cheek with gentle fingers.

"You were doomed," he said. "Long before I met you."

The horrible logic of the scheme dawned on me. It was diabolical. It was clever. I could see how it would work. Derek would be accused of murder, and the police would find two bodies in the cellars. Only a madman could have conceived the scheme. Only a madman could have carried it out with such cool deliberation. Alex was mad. I had been bewitched by his boyish charm, drawn by his magnetic appeal, but that was a cover for the real man, the man who revealed himself only in the sensational pages of his bloodthirsty, sadistic books.

He was standing very close to me. I could feel the warmth of his body and smell the odor of him. I stared over his shoulder at the yellow light flickering on the wet stone walls. Black shadows danced there in bizarre patterns, dark demons celebrating this evil. The currents of icy air swirled down the passage, making soft, whispering noises. I was about to die. It was not real. It couldn't be real.

Alex heaved his chest. He stood back a little and rubbed his thumb along his lower lip, his eyes pensive. He seemed to be deliberating the best way to kill me. I leaned against the wall, watching him, unable to do anything but study the features of his face. The evil was there now, the charming mask abandoned.

"You . . . you can do it," I said.

"But of course I can."

"You won't . . . you won't get away with it."

"Deborah, don't speak in clichés. Of course I'll get away with it. There is absolutely nothing to associate me with the crimes—besides my brief public association with you. When it all comes out, I'll be very shocked. I'll tell them the truth—part of it, at least. I'll say you believed my cousin had murdered Delia, that you were looking for proof. I'll hammer the last nail in Derek's coffin. So you see, it all works out, smooth, perfect. I've disposed of both problems, Tottie dead and Derek imprisoned for the rest of his life. Nice."

"You're insane," I whispered.

"They say genius is akin to madness. Perhaps you're right. Surely you'll concede the genius of the plot. There'll be no loose ends and no clumsy errors."

"Delia—"

"Tottie," he corrected. "Tottie and I are leaving for Italy first thing in the morning. She doesn't know we're going yet, but I'll convince her the trip is necessary—a break, a holiday. A week from now I'll return, alone. Who cares about a vulgar little barmaid? I'll say she ran off with a wine merchant, deserted me. They will have started searching for you by the time I get back. Perhaps they will have found you."

"You intend to kill her, too."

"It's reasonable, isn't it?"

"Reasonable? You *are* mad."

He sighed wearily. Telling me his scheme in its every detail had given him great satisfaction. He had been able to flaunt and brag about his "brilliance," and his own words had nourished his warped ego. Now the time for talk was over. He was weary of it. In the flickering glow of the oil lamp his face was diabolically handsome, diabolically evil. His wide mouth was still spread in the fixed smile, and there was a dark glitter in his eyes.

"I've left nothing out," he said, "forgotten nothing."

"You forgot this," I said.

I pointed the gun at his chest.

"I'll shoot," I said. My voice trembled.

He reached over and took the gun from my hand.

"Don't be absurd," he said. "You surely didn't think it was loaded? Grant me that much intelligence."

"You were playing with me—all along. The protests, the warnings, the concern for my welfare . . ."

"Of course I was playing with you. It gave me great pleasure. You were so very predictable, Deborah. I knew you'd never think to check and see if the gun was loaded. I knew you were headstrong, bold. I knew if I warned you to take no risks you'd go ahead anyway and act like one of the heroines I'd compared you to."

"You can't—"

"No one saw me come here. No one knows, besides Delia. She thinks I've come to tell you the whole story —which I have. I repeat, no one saw me come. Perhaps you've heard about the secret passage. I came in through it." He indicated the huge room at the end of the passageway, the room where I had found the scarf. The currents of icy air were coming from there, and I knew he must have opened a secret door. "In the woods on the other side of the gardens, there's a crevice in the side of the hill. It opens onto a tunnel that comes out in the room. I used it before, when I planted the scarf. I'll go back the way I came. No one will be any the wiser. Now, Deborah, the time has come—"

I stared at him, unable to speak, unable to move.

"Something dramatic, I think," he said quietly. He might have been selecting a suitable tie. "Something heinous—the public taste for gore and sensation must be appeased. I'm going to give them what they want: a treacherous villain—Derek; a beautiful heroine—you; and a crime so foul they'll shudder as they relish every detail of it in the tabloids." He ran his thumb along his lip, thinking. "It must be perfect—"

He seized me, his hands gripping my arms. He pulled me to him, and when he spoke again his lips were close to my ear. He crooned, as though the thing he was describing was beautiful and soothing and I was a child he was explaining it to.

"The cell," he said. "Yes, ideal. There are chains, manacles. I will chain you to the wall and leave you. I'll lock the door of the cell behind me, and you'll die. It'll be slow. You'll scream at first. You will cling to the thought that someone will come, someone will save you, but no one will come—why should they? What would they be doing in this part of the cellars? After a while, you won't be able to scream. You'll find it hard to breathe. There'll be hunger, and thirst, and finally, there'll be nothing but the prayer for death."

He swirled me around and began to push me toward the door of the cell. He was amused. The smile curled pleasantly, and his eyes were filled with dancing delight. I struggled. He didn't seem to notice. He was strong. His madness gave him an extra strength that made my efforts to escape futile, the thrashings of an animal in a steel trap. Alex was chuckling softly to himself as he thrust me into the room. I fell to the floor. I could see his dark silhouette standing there in the doorway, his chest heaving, his clenched fists hanging at his sides.

"That'll be enough, Alex," the voice said.

Alex turned, a look of total horror on his face.

The blow landed on the side of his head. He hurtled backward. The glow of the lamp flickered, danced madly, throwing weird shadows across the walls. I climbed to my feet. I stumbled to the door. I clung to the frame and watched the macabre ballet. I saw the flailing arms, heard the sharp impact of crashing blows, saw the bodies clinging together, swaying, falling. They were dark shapes, rolling, panting, crushing, and it seemed they moved in slow motion. I could see no features, no clear outlines, just the dark, grappling shapes and their wild shadows thrown against the wall by the flickering yellow light.

They struggled to their feet. I watched the shadows. I saw the arm swing back, saw it make contact, saw the other shape crash against the wall and slowly slip to the floor. I saw only the shadows, and it was not real. I heard the moan, the gasp. I looked away from the shadows. I looked at the man standing over that shape on the floor, saw him reach down and touch the face with a curiously gentle gesture.

"He cracked his skull against the wall. He's dead."

He was not speaking to me. He spoke to someone else, a man standing a few feet away.

"It's just as well," the man replied. "A blessing, really."

I tried to speak, but I was unable to. He came to me, and I collapsed into his arms. He held me for a long time, his hand stroking my hair, his arms nestling me loosely against him.

I looked up at his grim face. I trembled.

"He—"

"We heard it all. We were standing just outside the

circle of light all the time. This is Martin Craig, the friend I called the first morning you were here. He came down today. We have all the evidence we need. A few minutes ago Alex unknowingly clarified everything we weren't sure about."

"Martin Craig—" I whispered.

"He's been working on it ever since I called. I talked to him this morning, twice. He flew down this afternoon when he was sure. Alex was not as careful as he thought. Several people saw him with your cousin—he courted her in secret, but she was too well known not to be spotted."

"You were there—while he . . ."

"We had to let him talk. We had to know all the details."

"It was—"

"Don't try to talk now," Derek Hawke said. His guttural voice was harsh, but there was a gentle tone in it that I had never heard before. "Come," he said.

"It wasn't you . . ."

"Come," he repeated. "It's over now, truly over. Delia is waiting for you upstairs."

20

"I'll be thankful to Freddie Jay for the rest of my life," Delia said. "He's such a *crashing* bore, and I really can't abide him, but just the same, I owe him my life, you might say."

"You might," I replied.

"If he hadn't seen us together in that dreary little pub! Alex was so *secretive*. I couldn't imagine why he didn't want anyone to know about us. There was the book, of course, and tricking you, but I couldn't see why we had to sneak around all that time in London. I mean, we weren't doing anything *dishonest*—after all. Not that *I* knew of."

"Well—" I began.

"Oh, Debbie, don't. It was such fun. You know how I loved all his books, and he was so fascinating. I thought I was helping him with the book, really doing something constructive for once in my life instead of wearing spangles and making faces and dancing. If only I had known—"

She shuddered. All the brightness went out of her pixie face. She reached for my hand and squeezed it, and for a moment we remembered together, and we were very close, two against the world. Delia shook her head, and I smiled.

"It's over," I said. "Freddie Jay saw you and Alex at the pub two days before you left London, and he told Martin Craig about it, and the detective was able to put two and two together, with Derek's help."

"Yes," she said. "Derek—"

She grinned impishly and looked at me with mischievous eyes. I refused to make any comment. We were sitting at a table on the terrace behind the inn. There were small trees in large white pots, and beyond the railing the river flowed like a sparkling blue ribbon. It was the middle of the afternoon, four days after Alex's death, and up in our room the bags were packed. Delia had flatly refused to drive back to London in my old car. It was in a garage now, getting a new set of tires and a complete overhaul. The mechanic would deliver it to me in a few days. We were taking a train to London, and it would leave at six o'clock. We had come out here for a final cup of tea.

The case was closed now. We could leave.

We had had to remain in Hawkestown until it was all settled. We had both undergone long interviews with various men from Scotland Yard, and we had both waited apprehensively for the newspapers to break the story. It was a small story, unsensational. Derek Hawke still had several connections in high places, and he had used all his influence to keep the more lurid aspects of the crime out of the papers. Delia's name was not mentioned, nor was mine. Only a few people knew the truth, and they were adhering to those traditional British characteristics—absolute silence and stoical reserve.

Delia had brought me to the inn that night after Alex's death. It would have been impossible for me to stay at Blackcrest any longer. I wanted only to forget the place and forget the horror I had known there, and now that the case was officially closed, I intended to go back to the city with Delia. She had wired her agent three days ago, and he was impatient for her to get back to London. A new revue was being cast. The producer wanted Delia. She was elated. She would go back in triumph, be very secretive when people asked about her "marriage," and in a few weeks she would be wearing spangles again and making faces and giving pleasure to hundreds of theatergoers as she cavorted behind the footlights.

I was not so elated.

Sooner or later, I would find another job. My face was definitely not my fortune, but it would do for more beer advertisements or serve to herald the virtues of a certain deodorant on tube-station placards. The prospects were hardly glorious, and I felt a curious sadness as I sat on the terrace and watched the river sparkle white and blue in the heavenly afternoon sunlight.

I had seen Derek Hawke only once, when I went to Honora's funeral. He stood beside Andrea at the graveside, holding her arm. She was wearing black veils, her face covered, but his face had been grim, chiseled from hard granite. I wondered if he felt guilty about Honora's death. I knew now that he had had her welfare in mind all along. He had been the only one who knew Neil for what he really was, and because of it he had had to play the stern patriarch.

That she had died never knowing he had been protecting her made the tragedy all the more poignant.

He nodded to me as we were leaving the graveside, a sober nod. I wiped the tears from my eyes and laid a single rose on the grave before the last car left that bleak cemetery in the country.

"Don't you think so?" Delia asked.

"What?" For a moment I had lost track of what she was saying.

"Dear, you haven't been listening. I've been going slightly mad over the man, praising him to the skies, and you've been daydreaming. He *is* madly attractive in a stern, rocky way, so virile and foreboding. If a man like that were interested in *me*, I'd be sitting on his doorstep night and day."

"What makes you think he's interested in me?"

"He kissed you."

"In a moment of distress, under strain."

"Come, now! He kissed you because he couldn't help himself. You've always been a ninny where men are concerned, Debbie. Admit it. You said yourself he was the most magnetic man you've ever met."

"He's not interested in women," I said primly.

"Ha!" she cried. "You're not going to hand me *that*. I saw his face that night he brought you up from the cellars. Who do you think you're kidding?"

"Just the same—"

"He's interested, Debbie. Believe me!"

"Well, I'm not. I found him thoroughly detestable— even if he did save my life. He's arrogant, and rude, and hard, and—"

Delia yawned gracefully, lifting her hand to stifle it. " 'The lady doth protest too much, methinks,' " she quoted.

"I don't intend to argue, Delia," I said, finding it hard to hide my irritation. "What you say might be true. He might be violently interested. He might want to swoop me up in his arms and ride off with me into a Technicolor sunset, but I'm not at all concerned. I have my career to think about."

"Your career!" Delia exclaimed. Her laughter tinkled in the air, merry silver notes that brought a flush to my cheeks. "Really, Debbie," she said. "Neither of us has ever had many illusions about *that.*"

"You don't have to be *bitchy* about it," I snapped.

Delia smiled her radiant smile and stood up. She lifted her wrist and glanced at the fragile silver watch. There was a secretive look in her eyes that I didn't like at all. She looked like the proverbial cat who has swallowed the canary, and I had learned long ago to beware when she had that look.

"I think I'll toddle along upstairs," she said. "Good luck."

"Good luck? What do you mean?"

"You're so bloody uninterested, and he'll be here in a minute. He called this afternoon while you were down at the desk. I told him he'd find you out here on the terrace."

"Delia," I cried.

She went on toward the door, moving with that jaunty grace that so enchanted her public. Her short red curls blazed in the sunlight, and at the door she turned to grin and give me a final wave. I sat at the table, fuming. It was hard to stay irritated with Delia. She was like a mischievous child, delighted with her own pranks. I sipped my tea and watched the river. I heard his footsteps as he walked across the terrace toward me.

"Thinking?" he said.

I looked up. He swung out the chair Delia had been sitting in and sat down in it himself. He propped his elbows on the table and stared at me. He wore the green corduroy jacket with leather patches over a white polo shirt. His tanned face looked tired. I knew he had been through a lot these past days, settling everything, yet despite the heavy lines of fatigue, there was a relaxed, mellow look about his face that had not been there before. A lock of hair had tumbled over his forehead, and his wide mouth was grinning. He stared at me rudely, saying nothing more. I felt a faint blush coloring my cheeks.

"Delia tells me your bags are packed," he said finally.

"They are, as a matter of fact."

"Good. I can put them in the car."

"The porter will see that they get to the station," I said coldly.

"Oh, but you're not going to the station. Didn't you know?"

"I beg your pardon?"

"You're coming to Blackcrest with me."

"I most certainly am not!"

"I'm tired," he said. "I don't feel like arguing. The house is grim and solemn now. It needs you. Andy needs you. It's going to be hard for her to get over all this, and the only thing that'll help is for her to get right back to those damned memoirs and work. You'll have to work twice as hard, be twice as bright and diverting. With your help, she'll snap out of it and be her old self. She's already asking for you. I told her I'd bring you back."

"That isn't fair!" I cried. "Using Andy to induce me

to come back! It's wicked, in fact. You know how fond of her I am. You know I couldn't stand to leave thinking she wanted me."

"Very wicked," he agreed. "I play dirty."

"Well, I don't intend to go back," I said firmly.

"Deborah—" he said.

His dark eyes looked into mine. There was a dancing light in them, and the grin on his mouth spread. It was infuriating.

"Blackcrest needs me. Andy needs me! Do you think that's enough to induce me to toss everything else aside and bury myself in the country and sleep in a *tower* and—"

"No," he said calmly, "but there are other inducements."

"Oh?"

He nodded slowly, his heavy lids drooping sheepishly over the dark black eyes.

"Such as?" I snapped.

"We'll discuss them later," he replied. "In great detail."

I stood up abruptly. My chair scraped loudly on the wooden floor as I pushed it away from the table. Derek looked at me with surprise, and then he stood up too. He moved with a lazy deliberation. I knew it was useless to fight him—or myself—any longer.

"Where are you going?" he asked. His voice was gruff.

"I . . . I'm going to tell Delia to cancel my train reservation."

I stared at Derek Hawke for a moment. The blush still burned on my cheeks. He stood with his hands in his pockets, his shoulders hunched up. Relief had flooded his face, and he was smiling as I had never seen him smile before. He had won, as he had known all along he would.

"Make it quick," he said.

"I don't like to be rushed," I retorted.

"Too bad. I don't intend to waste any more time."

"Don't you?"

"Not a minute," Derek Hawke replied.